Endless Lies

Ella Miles

LIES SERIES

Lies We Share: A Prologue

PROLOGUE
CORBIN

REVENGE.

It's all I can think about. It's the only thing keeping me sane, keeping me breathing, keeping me alive.

The amount of loss my family has endured is too much. The pain destroyed us all. It turned me into a hollow shell, with nothing but a black heart left beneath my ribs. It turned my brother into a fighter intent on killing. It turned my other brother into a hardened soul who will never let anyone in. And my sister has become a woman whose only wish is for death.

I have no doubt that my actions will do little to heal any of us, but that isn't my intention. We are all broken souls, all heartless. There is no fixing people who have been touched by the absolute worst darkness in the world.

Revenge isn't about us; it's about destroying those who unleashed the darkness onto the world, but who we can stop from causing further carnage.

As I take a step into blindingly white hallways filled with people rummaging about in and out of hospital rooms, I know this is the first step toward getting our revenge.

The bastard thinks I'm working for him because I'm a greedy asshole who will do anything for money. He thinks I'm broke and need to get in his good graces to rebuild my family. He doesn't realize I'm working for him to gain the tools to destroy him.

There is a nurses' station that I'll have to get past before I can reach Liesel's room. I play my options in my head. Pretend to be the father or other family member. Pretend to work here. Flirt my way through. Or use the threat of danger.

It turns out I don't have to use any of those strategies. As I approach the nurses' station, an alarm sounds.

"Code blue!" someone yells, and everyone scatters to the room on the far end of the hallway.

Quite convenient—unless it's the room I'm here for.

I scan the board behind the desk and find names attached to rooms. Liesel Dunn is in room 302.

I snag one of the hospital bands for guests and slap it on my wrist. I begin to make my way toward room 302, but I immediately stop.

There is a man outside the room pacing back and forth.

The father?

No, this man is barely more than a boy. The man who raped Liesel is much older. This boy's brow is covered in sweat, his eyebrows are raised in worry, and his entire body is tense and flustered.

He's muttering words to himself and doesn't notice my presence.

There's a scream coming from the room that draws his attention to the door. He stops abruptly like his heart just stopped at the sound of the woman's screams.

I hate to admit it, but my heart flutters too. The sound the woman is making is not that much different than

Phoenix's wail of agony the day her triplets were born lifeless.

Is the woman losing her baby?

I want to run inside to see. If she is, then my plan is ruined. But this damn man is standing in the way. I could take him. He's nothing but a scrawny boy, and in his state, I doubt he'd put up much of a fight. But I don't want to draw any unwanted attention.

Suddenly, a doctor and a nurse push past the boy, not giving him a second look as they enter the room. Their voices are quick as they explain what's happening.

C-section.

Perfect, it will be easier for me to take the baby if Liesel is unconscious. They will have to move the baby to the nursery. The plan continues to form in my head.

The boy's face is white as a ghost. He's terrified. And yet, he's too afraid to go into the room. What he's afraid of, I don't know, but it's clear he loves the girl in the room.

You shouldn't—I'm about to destroy her world, just like she and her father destroyed mine.

Suddenly, the doors to the girl's room are flung open, and her hospital bed is being rolled out.

The boy jumps back, turning down the hallway before she can get a glimpse of him.

She's writhing in pain in the bed. Her large belly is shifting even though contractions are no longer needed to get the baby out. She's gripping the railing of the bed so hard that her fingertips have turned white. She lets out a low, guttural growl as another contraction sweeps through her.

Her eyes glare at me as I realize I'm standing in the middle of the hallway in the direction the doctors are turning her bed.

I jump out of the way.

No one questions my presence here. They are too worried about getting her to surgery.

I watch as they begin to turn the corner with her, and I look back at the boy. I expect him to be staring at her, to be running after her, but he's gone—vanished.

Strange.

I watch as the doctor uses a badge to get through the doors to the surgery wing.

I glance in the other direction toward the room at the far end where all the commotion was. Nurses and doctors have started to file back out of the room and head back to their usual stations. They all look exhausted but relieved. Whoever was in that room is still alive.

But they are distracted.

I walk purposefully toward them until I knock into one of the women.

"Sorry," I mutter.

She smiles at me and then turns abruptly when she gets a look at my eyes. She sees the wickedness in the way they gleam at her, and she's smart enough to know that despite my good looks, she shouldn't get involved.

I cling her stolen badge in my fingertips and head toward the waiting room.

I don't know how long it takes to deliver a baby via c-section, but I suspect I have a few minutes. I need the baby alive, so I need to let the doctors do their jobs.

After sucking down coffee and seeing some of the nurses that headed back with Dunn reemerge, I decide the baby must be born.

I walk through the door, quickly scanning the nurse's badge. Past the surgery door, I see Liesel still lying on the operating table. I notice the boy is looking through a door's glass on the other side of the room.

Interesting, maybe he's smarter than I thought.

The boy is focused on the girl, not the baby. He doesn't see the nurse rolling the baby out of the room and into the hallway.

Here's my chance.

The woman turns the small incubator, and I gasp at the sight.

There isn't just one baby.

There are three babies.

Plural.

I glance around, looking for the source of the other babies. *Did another woman deliver her babies recently as well?*

But they wouldn't put all three babies together if they weren't siblings, would they?

The nurse stops when she spots me with my jaw dropped on the floor.

She smiles sweetly at me.

"You must be the father," she says.

"Uh-huh," I say back.

"Follow me, and I can take you to a room where you can meet your new babies."

I don't move, so the woman walks over to me and takes my hand. "I'm Anne."

I nod.

Then she's holding my hand while pushing the cart of three babies.

Three.

Babies.

What the hell am I supposed to do with three?

The woman leads me into a small room.

"Liesel needs to go to recovery first, and then she'll be brought in, probably in about an hour. I can take the babies to the nursery for you, but I thought you might like a private room to be introduced."

"The babies—are they…?"

"They are all perfectly healthy. Usually, with triplets, we expect at least one or more to have to spend time in the NICU, but Liesel did an excellent job keeping these babies safe."

Three babies. I still can't wrap my head around it.

The woman must be used to shocked dads because my expression doesn't even phase her.

"Sit down on the bed," she says.

I don't know why she wants me to sit on the hospital bed in the room. Maybe she thinks I'm going into shock?

I sit on the edge. "I'm fine, really."

She smiles, shaking her head. "Get all the way in the bed."

I frown but do as she says.

I watch as she picks up the first baby and walks over to me, placing the baby in my arms without question. Then she does the same for the second and the third until I'm holding all three babies.

"See? It's not so hard. You got this, father. You've got two strong boys, and your baby girl has one hell of a pair of lungs on her."

I look down at them—two boys, one girl.

"I'll leave you alone to get acquainted with your new babies. I'll be back in twenty minutes to do another health check on them, but press the call button on the bed railing if you need any help."

And then she's gone.

My eyes are wide as I look at each of the tiny infants in my arms. All of them are in various states of sleep. Thank god, because I don't know what I'd do if they started crying or begging for food. I know the nurse thought she was giving me a sweet moment alone with my babies, but how ignorant of her to think that I would know what to do. She didn't even check my bracelet; she just assumed that since I was a man outside of surgery that I must be the father.

"What do I do with the three of you?" I say, looking at each of them.

I remember Mr. Dunn's words. *If the baby is a girl, kill her. If it's a boy, bring him to me.*

I stare at each of them as a plan forms in my head. *Maybe one of us can heal after all? And sooner than I think.*

Carefully, I stand up, balancing the three babies in my arms. I lay them down on the bed. I don't know much about babies, but I don't think they can move or roll much at this age, so I'm not too worried about them falling off the bed.

I walk over to the computer in the corner and use my badge to scan in. I want to make Liesel and her father suffer, and the best way to do that is to kill them—all of them.

But since I have no intention of actually killing the babies, I'll just make them think they are dead.

I pull up Liesel's chart and start typing furiously in, trying to sound as medical and objective as I can so my ruse will be believed.

I type out the babies died just after birth. The funeral home already received them for cremation.

Now, to get out of here without being seen.

One baby would be hard enough to sneak out, but three? It's going to be impossible.

I unzip my jacket before snuggling two of the babies inside. The third I scoop up and hold in my hands.

My objective is to exit the building as fast as I can. I saw an emergency exit stairwell at the end of the hall—that's my goal.

I run out into the hallway, jogging fast and determined— so fast I don't notice the boy rounding the corner. I smack into him. The baby in my hands falls into his arms.

He catches the baby, completely confused.

I make a rash decision. The boy doesn't know there are three babies. I can still get out of here with the other two.

"Congratulations on becoming a father," I say, and then I run out the exit door and down the stairs, cradling the two babies beneath my jacket.

I burst through the final door and out into the bright sunlight before jogging to my truck.

No sooner have I climbed into the car do I hear him.

"Did you do it? Do you have the baby?" Mr. Dunn asks from behind me.

Fuck.

Of course, he didn't think I was loyal to him. He needed to be here to ensure I behaved and did as I was told.

Both babies are somehow still asleep beneath my jacket.

I consider my options carefully.

I can still get away with keeping one—the girl.

I can give him the boy.

I don't have a choice.

Reluctantly, I reach into my jacket and spot the blue blanket surrounding the boy. I pull him out and hand him to the dangerous man behind me.

"You—you aren't going to kill him, are you?" I ask, even though I know it's not my place, and he probably won't answer me.

"Why would I kill such a perfect boy? He's going to ensure my name lives on."

Then he climbs out of the car with the boy I had no intention of giving up.

I'll get him back, I vow. The kids are all innocent. Mr. Dunn and his daughter are not.

Liesel has the other boy.

I'll get them all back.

I'll get my revenge.

For now, my sister has a child to raise. A child who might help her heal.

1

LANGSTON

My body bounces harshly in the front seat of the truck. My body thumps into the window as my ass rises and falls with the truck taking the bumps too quickly.

"You still with me?" Maxwell asks from the driver's seat.

"Like you give a damn if I live or die."

"I do, actually, since it's my job to keep you alive long enough to deliver you back to your friends. After that, I don't give a damn if what you do."

"Turn us around and go back to the airport. I need to get back to Liesel."

Maxwell laughs. "If I turn this car around or slow down in the slightest, you won't be breathing long enough to get back to Liesel. Your only chance of ever seeing her again is to get back to your friends and hope they have a surgeon ready like I told them to."

"I'm fine. I'm not in any pain; the wound can't be that bad."

"That's because we pumped you with so many pain meds you're high as a kite and can't make decisions for yourself. That's why Liesel had to rescue your ass, again."

I curse under my breath but stop arguing with him. It's not going to do any good. I can barely feel my toes, let alone do I have the energy to attack Maxwell and take control of the car to get back to Liesel. I need to spend my time thinking, preparing for when I regain control of my body.

I think back to being on the plane, to the conversation Liesel and Corbin had. *What deal did Liesel make with Corbin? What did she trade in exchange for my life? For our kids' lives?*

She already gave up her ability to have future kids. Both by taking some kind of poison and then again with the knife she forced into her lower abdomen. She wasn't pregnant. Liesel is a lot of things, but she would never kill her own child to save another. She wasn't pregnant like I thought.

I need to go back to get her, to tell her to hell with the treasure. It's not worth it. We need to kill all these motherfuckers. The people who are still loyal to her father even though he's dead. If we kill them, everyone will think we got and safely secured the treasure. They will stop attacking us, and our kids will be safe. That's all that matters.

Liesel seems to know more than I do, though. She's smart —that's why I call her the huntress. She's always searching, hunting, figuring things out long before I do. I'm the muscle, the killer, the one who finishes what she starts. She should know that she can't kill all these people by herself, though.

Maybe killing them isn't her plan? It's already clear she thinks Phoenix deserves to live. She's going soft and going to let them all live after what they've done. That's why she needs me to do the work she can't, and shouldn't, do herself.

"Take me back," I say again, as firmly as I can.

"I can't," Maxwell says, not looking in my direction. I can see the vein in his neck bulging, the shape of his brow dipping, his jaw clenched. Something has him stressed. *Is it the fact that he's on my island and about to be vastly outnumbered?*

10

"You can. I promise to make your death quick if you take me back. Otherwise, I'm drawing out the torture for years before I kill you."

He shakes his head. "Trust me; you don't want to go back."

"Why not?"

"Do you love Liesel?"

"Of course."

"Then, you can't go back. You don't have all the facts. Liesel does. Or she will shortly. You can't go back."

"Why not?"

"For one thing, she'll hate you, and all of this will be for nothing." Maxwell looks at me now. "Shit."

His eyes bulge as he looks at me, and he turns the wheel of the car sharply, driving us off the edge of the road.

I turn my head looking out the window behind me, expecting to see someone attacking us. But I don't see anything but darkness descending around us.

Maxwell throws his seatbelt off, and then he's reaching behind my seat and pulling a bag into his lap.

"Take some slow, deep breaths for me," Maxwell says.

"I'm fine."

"You're not fine. Your face is blue, and I'm pretty sure you have some internal bleeding causing havoc. If I don't do something to stop it, you're going to bleed out in my fucking truck. Which, as I told you earlier, is not going to fucking happen on my watch."

He leans over and examines my head more closely. Then he reaches behind my neck.

"Shit," he says again. He pulls a couple of items out of his bag. "I think the first problem is the back of your neck. I don't know how I didn't notice the blood spilling out from the back of your head."

"I'm not bleeding."

11

"You're delusional."

If I really am bleeding as badly as Maxwell's eyes and tone of voice are telling me, then I'm fucked. There is nothing Maxwell is going to be able to do to fix it.

Maxwell's mind whirls as he tries to think about what to do to stop the bleeding. A piece of gauze isn't going to work, and neither is stitching it up.

"This is going to hurt," is the only warning he gives me before he jabs something into my neck.

"Fuck!" The pain finally registers, rattling through my whole body and reminding me how nice it was to feel nothing before. "You stabbed me."

Maxwell ignores me, studying my neck where there is now a blunt object protruding.

"Don't move your head. Don't rest it on the headrest. Don't fucking die. Sound good?"

"Why are you helping me?"

He doesn't answer. He just starts driving again. Now, I think there really is more that he's not telling me.

"You shouldn't have fallen in love with her," he says.

"I know. I should have hated her, but she's too easy to love."

Maxwell shakes his head. "Just don't die."

"After I'm fixed, then will you take me to where Corbin has taken her? Or are you going to make us torture the location out of you?"

"Neither. You can't go to her. You know that. Her father's men will attack you and kill you both if you continue on with her. And you wouldn't dare risk her life."

"Then I'll send Enzo, Zeke, and Beckett."

"No, you won't, because they'll do the same thing to them."

"And you don't think they won't do the same thing to Corbin?"

"No."

"Well, he can't help her anyway. Only the man who married her can help her get the treasure."

I stare at Maxwell. "Don't tell me Corbin's plan is to get her to divorce me and then marry her himself."

"No, that's not his plan."

"Then, how does he think he'll be able to help her?"

"He just can. You don't need to worry about the details. Liesel already understands, and she agreed. If you won't listen to me, you need to listen to her for once in your life, or your kids are going to end up completely parentless."

I growl at the mention of my kids.

"Your kids are safe as long as you stay with them and let Liesel keep her end of the bargain. She doesn't need your help. She's got this. Loving her will just put her life in more danger."

"I can't un-love her. It's not possible."

"Well, it would help her most if you could figure out how to un-love her and prove it to the world. That's the only way to help her now."

I frown.

I'm going to get more information from him. As soon as I don't have to have a knife sticking out of the back of my neck in order to keep me alive, he's a dead man. So are his sister and brother and anyone else who has threatened our kids' lives.

We pull up in front of my beach house. All of my friends start running from the house toward us.

I smirk at Maxwell. "You better start talking, or they are going to kill you. You're the reason Siren may never talk again, Zeke may never hear again, and Beckett may never touch again. They aren't a forgiving bunch. And as you said, I'll be in surgery and not able to convince them to keep you alive until you tell us where Corbin and Liesel went."

"They already know. I already told them."

"What?"

My door is thrown open, and Enzo and Zeke are grabbing me, trying to figure out how to move me without injuring me more so they can take me to a room I'm sure they've set up for surgery. But I need more information from Maxwell before I'm put under. I implore Maxwell to talk to me with my eyes as my jaw is currently on the floor from what he just said.

Maxwell leans over so only I can hear his next words. "You want me and my family dead, but you shouldn't. Just maybe, we are all on the same side."

Then I'm whisked away by my friends, away from my ability to question Maxwell further. Darkness overcomes me before my brain can even process how there is a possibility that we are all on the same side.

Stop loving her. If you want to save her, then never love her. The words her father spoke to me all those years ago are the last thing in my brain before I'm unconscious.

2

LIESEL

We check into a hotel in Singapore. It's a penthouse with dozens of rooms, modern appliances, a jacuzzi tub, and a hundred-inch flatscreen in almost every room. You wouldn't want to be in a room where you couldn't not soak and fill your brain with constant television.

Corbin and I have an uneasy truce, so it's shocking to not see any of his security team in the hotel room and in the hallway.

"Where is your team?" I ask.

"I don't need a team. It's just you and I."

"You don't think I'll run?" I say, running my hand over the leather of the couch in one of this suite's two living rooms.

"No, you won't run. You know I'm your only hope of finding Declan and keeping those you love alive. If you run, our deal is off, and I'll go after your kids, as was my initial plan. Alas, I've gone soft. I want you to suffer, not your kids."

"You do realize your beef is with my father, not me, right? I've only met my father once."

Corbin puts his hands in the pockets of his black jacket. "I know, but your father is dead. It's only fair that you pay for his sins."

I shiver as he stares at me.

"So once this is all over, you're going to keep me as your sex slave until I eventually die?"

"Would it be so bad? If I remember correctly, you were the one who willingly sucked my cock."

"I did that to get the next clue. To find my child! Not because I enjoyed it, you fucking pig!"

He smirks, enjoying seeing me rattled up. "I don't want you as a sex slave. I have other plans for you."

He walks over to his suitcase and pulls something out before handing it to me. It's a first aid kit and a change of clothes. My clothes are bloodied, and I still have an open wound from where I stabbed myself.

I take the clothes and head into one of the six bathrooms in the penthouse hotel. I don't know why Corbin decided to get us such an expensive hotel for the night. It makes me nervous about what is going to happen next.

I shower, tend to my wound, and get dressed quickly. Every second we waste is another second my son is in danger.

He could be dead, that voice in my head says. If he is, everything we've all sacrificed for would be for nothing.

He's not dead. I refuse to believe Declan is dead.

I step back out into the living room where I left Corbin, but I don't find him.

"Corbin?" I ask, shouting down the hallway, and my ears turned up trying to listen for him. I half expect him to have brought his entire team up to the floor while I was in the shower. Instead, I find him out on the large patio that overlooks the city with a drink in one hand.

His eyes scan me up and down, but not in a hungry way. It's annoyed, more in a way that tells me I interrupted him deep in thought.

"What were you thinking about?" I ask.

He motions for me to sit, and he takes the chair opposite mine. Most outdoor furniture is stiff and scratchy, but this chair feels like I'm sitting on a cloud.

"Your father," he says. He finishes his drink, once again staring off into the distance. I don't think he's going to tell me whatever he's thinking about, but then he turns back.

"I think it's time you and I tell each other everything we know."

"You go first," I say.

"I will because you need to realize that we aren't on different sides, you and I."

"I sold my soul to you in order to keep my children and husband safe. I think you and I are on as far of opposite sides as we can possibly get."

"You're wrong."

"Tell me about my father."

"When I first met your father, I thought he was a nothing. I thought he had a few connections to drug dealers, but I didn't think he was much more. He didn't seem that powerful. Honestly, I thought he was an addict himself. He was always a bit on edge, twitchy, with red shot eyes. Realizing I misjudged him cost me everything." He balls his hands into fists, full of anger and frustration at himself as much as my father.

He's silent for a while and then nods his head in my direction. I realize he's expecting me to tell him what I know about my own father.

"You know more than me. He didn't raise me. I only met him once, and it was to tell me about the fucking treasure, the bastard. He's the one who took two of my kids from me, wasn't he?" I don't know why I expect Corbin to know, except that he actually knew him. They worked together.

"Yes, he took Rose and Declan."

"Why only take two and not all three?"

"Because your father wanted an heir to his operations. He knew no daughter of his would ever be strong enough. And after you were born, he suffered an injury that prevented him from having kids after you. So he waited until you had kids of your own. He took Declan because he was the strongest, the healthiest, and he thought he could raise him to become his heir."

"So my father's people have Declan now?" I ask, although I already know this. I just need Corbin to confirm it for me again.

He nods once solemnly.

"Why take Rose? He obviously didn't keep her?"

"Because daughters were weak. He didn't want you to raise a daughter. He ordered his men to kill her, but evidently, that was a line that even his men couldn't cross."

"And Atlas? Why let me keep him?"

"He was the smallest, weakest, most fragile. I think he figured he'd die, but if he didn't, he'd have a backup heir to come after."

I tremble in my chair.

"You hate my father. You hate me. Why help me get Declan?"

Corbin fidgets in his chair as his eyes water.

"Wait...how do you know all of this about my father?"

"Because I worked for him. After the death of Martin and Phoenix's children, I signed up to work for him. I was the one who took your children with plans to kill them all. I couldn't, so I made a plan to give them to Phoenix to help

18

her heal and get her revenge for what she had lost. Your father intervened before I could enact my plan."

"You saved Rose instead of killing her?"

"Yes."

I frown. *Maybe we are on the same side after all.* No, he still demanded my body and soul in exchange for helping me. He still blames me. *But why does he blame me?* It has to be more than he's telling me.

And then it hits me.

"You want me separated from the kids so Phoenix can have them. You think with me out of the picture, she can be their mother instead of me. She can heal."

His eyes glaze over, but I know it's the truth. He feels guilty about her losing her babies, and this has always been about trying to remedy that.

Finally, he speaks again. "Falling in love was stupid. You could have gotten Declan back if you hadn't fallen in love. Now, I'm your only hope."

"I know falling in love was stupid, dangerous, cruel. I tried preventing myself from it almost my entire life. And even more, I tried to keep him from falling in love with me, but neither of us could help it. I think we fell in love when we were kids, the first time we met. Our hearts fell. Each one belonged to the other. It took years of fighting it before either of us admitted it out loud."

A tear rolls down my cheek. "What do we have to do next, or do you not know?"

"You're going to have to give him up, for real. You're going to have to stop loving him and get him to stop loving you. That's the only way to get Declan back."

I wipe my tears, not sure if he's answering my question or reacting to my comments from before.

"I know," I say because I want Langston to give me up. It's the only way to save him from so many terrible things.

His eyes search mine, sliding slowly back and forth like he's questioning if I'm strong enough to do it. Apparently, he's satisfied, and then he speaks words that send chills down my spine.

"Your father is alive. Declan is with him. We find your father; we get Declan back."

3

LANGSTON

I OPEN my eyes but don't feel anything.

Am I dead?

It would make sense if I were. I remember being whisked into a back room of the house where a surgery room had been set up. Bright lights shone down on me before I became unconscious. Some might think it's a sign that I'm in heaven, but I know better. If I'm dead, I'm definitely in hell.

I can't feel anything, though. I'm numb. I'm not in hell. If I were, I'd be in burning pain. Instead, the only thing I feel is an erratic heartbeat as I wait to find out if Liesel and my kids are safe. I haven't been here to protect them as I should. I have no idea how long I was unconscious; anything could have happened.

I feel a presence in the room but don't hear anything.

I turn my head and see Siren sitting next to my bed; a window that looks out to the ocean is behind her. It's a dreary looking day. The sun is barely poking through the clouds, and there is a light drizzle soaking the sand.

Siren takes my hand as we both take a deep inhale and exhale, both settling now that she knows I'm going to survive. I suspect nothing bad did happen while I was out since Siren is here and not trying to get someone else to come in and help her explain some atrocity that happened.

Even though Siren can't speak much right now, I don't need her to. And she doesn't need me to speak either. We've been through too much together. We share a connection that transcends the ability to speak. Right now, I'm thankful for that. I know I can use my voice, but I don't really want to speak.

"Safe," Siren finally speaks out. The one word is enough to confirm that everyone is safe. No one has been hurt while I was out.

I nod.

Her eyes scan over my body, taking in all my injuries, bandages, and scars. I let her, but I don't follow her gaze. I don't want to know all of my injuries. It makes no difference. All I really want right now is to talk to Maxwell and find out what he was talking about before I became unconscious. I want to find out why he thinks we are on the same side. But I don't know if he's even still here or if he's dead. I wouldn't put it past Enzo and Zeke to kill him. He deserves it.

Siren pats my hand again, drawing my attention back to her. Then she's hugging me tightly. I don't feel that either. I don't feel anything but my aching heart that's longing to be with Liesel. I don't care if we have to face a firing squad again; I'd rather be facing death with her than be without her.

Siren's eyes flick left and right over mine, searching for what I want. She sees whatever it is without having to ask. She holds up one finger and then walks out the door. I don't know what she saw or who is going to enter my room next. I expect a doctor to come in and examine me, to tell me the extent of my injuries. If it was Kai who was sitting next to me when I woke up, I would have no doubt that that is what is about to happen.

But the door opens, and Maxwell steps in instead.

I grin; Siren always knows me as well as I knew myself.

"You look like hell," he says as he walks near the queen-sized bed I'm lying in.

"It's your fault I look like this. You could have just left me for dead," I say.

He grins. "I could have, but then that would be breaking a deal. That's not something I do."

"A deal you made with Liesel to save my life?"

He nods.

"Why did you say we're on the same side when clearly we aren't? You're holding Liesel hostage. You tried to kill my family. You took my kids from me. You took Siren's voice, Zeke's hearing, Beckett's touch, Liesel's fertility. You've taken so much from all of us. Do you really think we can just forgive you and work on the same side?"

Maxwell doesn't take Siren's seat. He walks over to the window and looks out at the ocean, taking his sweet time. It's time we don't have. I want to jump out of this bed and force him to talk to me, but the numbness in my limbs hasn't vanished. There's an IV still in my arm pumping me with drugs, so I'm at his mercy.

"Have you figured out what the treasure is yet? Have you pieced it together?" he asks me.

I frown and shrug. "I assume an insane amount of money or gold or something stupid like that."

"No." Maxwell snaps his head back to look at me. "The treasure is Declan."

"What?"

"The treasure is Declan. We never had him; we just knew the way to get Declan was to solve the puzzle, the clues that Liesel's father left."

That's why Liesel made the trade—not only for my life but to ensure she saved Declan. All the more reason I should be by her side doing whatever it takes to save him with her.

"Her father is still alive," Maxwell says next.

"What? That's not possible. I buried that motherfucker. I stood at his grave. I—"

"It was an imposter—someone her father hired to pretend to be him. You've never actually met her father. Neither has she."

"That's not—I have to go to her. I have to help her! I can't stay here. If her father's alive, I—"

"Need to stay away from her. Her father hates you. Hates what you represent. He thinks you'll destroy his daughter and everything he built. If you go to Liesel, he'll attack you again."

"Fuck!" I yell, not sure what to do. I should try to contact Liesel at least to figure out what her plan is and how we can help. But I'm not sure how to contact her or if Corbin will let me talk to her.

"Corbin won't hurt her," Maxwell says.

"He has before."

"He won't now. He wants Declan as much as you do. He wants to take down her father as much as you do. He won't hurt her until that's done."

"And after? What then?"

Maxwell's silence answers for him. Once they save Declan and kill her father, Corbin will finish his revenge. Liesel saved my life in exchange for working with Corbin to get Declan back. *But what else did she trade? What else did she have to sacrifice?*

"What do you think I should do?" I ask.

Maxwell's brow furrows. "You do whatever it takes to keep Liesel safe while getting Declan back. You protect your family. You don't cower. You fight. But you don't let her father know that you're helping Liesel."

The corner of my mouth lifts; he's right. Maxwell seems to be the kind of man who will help me. We have an uneasy truce that I still don't understand or trust, but I'm going to need his help.

"I'll tell your friends that you're awake," Maxwell says, exiting the room.

When the door opens again, Atlas and Rose come running inside and jump on the bed before Phoenix can corral them.

I glare at Phoenix, who stands in the doorway. "Be gentle with your father. You don't want to hurt him more."

"Sorry," both kids say at the same time.

I smile at both of them sitting on my lap. "Don't be sorry. I missed you both so much."

I try to move my arms to squeeze them both, but they are so heavy I can barely lift them.

"Guys, give your dad a hug," Phoenix says, noticing that I can't give them one as I want.

The kids don't have to be told twice. They cling to my neck as my arms lift enough to pat them on their lower backs.

"You're going to be okay?" Atlas asks.

"Yes, I'm going to be just fine. I just had a car accident, so I'm a little beat up, but I'll survive."

"Good," Rose says.

"Do you want ice cream? Ice cream always helps," Atlas says.

"I'd love some ice cream or anything else you two make me."

"Come on, kids, let's go make some ice cream with Aunt Kai, and then we can let your dad rest," Phoenix says, letting me know that she's not been hanging out with the kids unsupervised. It's then that I spot Kai just outside the door-way, keeping an eye on Phoenix.

"What about our other mom? Is she coming back soon?" Rose asks.

I take a deep breath, stalling as I try to figure out how to answer.

"Your other mom is with your brother right now," I start. I hate calling Liesel their other mother when she is their mother and has sacrificed so much for them, while Phoenix has done nothing but use them. But I know it's what's for the best for the kids right now. They barely know Liesel, and Phoenix has done nothing but love them in their eyes.

"When will they be back?" Rose asks.

I squeeze them both. "I don't know, as soon as they can. They want to be with us very much but it's safer for them right now to not travel. As soon as they can though, they'll come here. I promise."

4

LIESEL

MY FATHER IS ALIVE.

For most people, hearing that a parent you thought was dead is, in fact, alive might bring joy. It might raise their spirit. They might race to go find them and regain the lost time.

Not for me.

For me, hearing my father has been alive this entire time and that I've never actually met him sends shockwaves through me.

The man I met, who gave me the letter, wasn't my father.

The man I buried wasn't my father.

I've always known my father was a cruel man. I just didn't realize he was worse than the devil.

My father is responsible for every horrible thing in my life. For the loss of time with my kids. For their kidnappings. For my enemies. For my pain. For the loss of Langston, I will surely endure. He's responsible for all of it.

I don't know why my father decided not to be in my life and yet ruin it entirely. *Why take my children from me? Why refuse me to love the only man in the world I ever could? Why control me without ever getting to know me?*

Because he's a wicked, evil man.

A man I now want dead.

I stare at Corbin across from me, still not sure if I should trust him or if I should run from him. But he seems to have information that I desperately need to find the last of my children. To kill my father and ensure my family's safety.

"What is the next clue?" I ask Corbin. My throat creaks as I speak.

Corbin studies me a moment before he speaks. "Are you ready to help me?"

"Since I have no information about where my father is, I don't know how I can help."

He pulls a card out of his pocket and hands it to me.

I take it carefully to ensure our fingers don't brush. I read the card, and it doesn't make sense. It might as well be gibberish or in a foreign language.

"What does this mean?"

"I was hoping you had the rest of the clue. I've spent the last few years trying to figure it out, but I haven't been able to."

I read the card over and over, trying to piece together what it could mean. I think back to the note that my father, well, the man pretending to be my father, gave me.

It hits me all at once.

"Moscow," I say.

Corbin's eyebrows jump up. "Moscow? Do you have more than that? Moscow's a big city."

I study the card again. "No, but I know who might."

Corbin narrows his eyes like he's not sure he believes I don't already know.

"Langston?" he finally asks.

I nod.

"Shit," he curses under his breath.

We are going to have to involve Langston in this. At least call and talk to him. Something I'm desperate to do anyway because the last time I saw him, he was pale and rapidly deteriorating. But I don't want him involved. Even calling Langston could decide his fate, and I won't allow him to die. He has to live at all costs. He has to be there for our children. He has to take care of them.

Before I contact him and get more information about our next step, putting his life in danger, I need more reassurance from Corbin that we are on the same side. If I do speak to Langston, I don't know if I can keep him from coming if he knows the location. I'll only work with Corbin if I know that Langston will be safe.

"I'll call Langston. I will figure out the rest of the clue, but I need some reassurances first."

Corbin cocks his head. "What makes you think you are in any place to negotiate?"

"You need me to get your revenge. You've had years to figure it out on your own, and you failed."

Corbin smirks. "As I said before, we are on the same side."

"Prove it." My eyes dig into his skin, threatening to end him.

Our eyes lock as he thinks about how he can prove his loyalty to me. I don't think he can. I don't think he will. I'll have to figure out how to save Declan, kill my father, and keep Langston alive by myself.

Corbin leans forward and reaches into his boot, pulling out a knife.

I don't recoil. I stay strong as I face my enemy, now holding a weapon he can use against me. I've been tortured enough to know that nothing he does to me will matter.

Corbin twists the knife around in his hand, taunting me

with how he'll use it on me. It makes no difference. I always knew I would die a horrible death. Today is as good a day as any, especially if it means Langston is safe. My father will have no reason to go after Langston if I'm dead.

"You sacrificed, your friends sacrificed, so I too shall sacrifice."

My eyes darken, not understanding what he's going to do. Suddenly, he plunges the knife into his stomach in a very similar spot to where I did.

He doesn't make a sound as the knife pierces his flesh. Nor does he moan as the blood oozes out after he's removed the blade. His piercing eyes remain on mine, judging if I'm happy enough with his sacrifice. His eyes tell me that if I'm not, that he'll do something else. If I asked him to cut off his own arm, he would.

If we really are going to be on the same side, then I need him as whole and uninjured as possible.

"Are you satisfied, or should I cut off an ear? An arm? A testicle?" He smirks at me, daring me to tell him to do more.

I've given him my life when this is all over. The more pain I inflict on him now, the worse he'll make my life later, I have no doubt. We are on the same side now with the same mission, but that won't always be the case. Although, watching him cut off a testicle could be entertaining.

"I'll go get the first aid kit," I say, accepting his sacrifice. His is small, a wound to the stomach, but for now, it's enough.

5

LANGSTON

Maxwell and I just landed in Singapore and are driving into the city. We don't know if Liesel and Corbin are still here, but this is the last place Maxwell knew, so this is where we'll start.

Saying goodbye to Rose and Atlas was heartbreaking even though they were happy to play with their aunts and uncles in their favorite place in the world. But every time I walk away from them, I don't know if I'll be going back. I don't know if it will be the last time I ever see them. It's the right thing to do; they deserve a mother. They deserve to have their brother. My risking my life is worth it, but it's still hard.

Watching them with Phoenix was harder. They still think of her as a loving mother, and she still acts like one. I don't know how I'm ever going to be able to remove her from their lives without destroying them, but that's a conversation for a later date.

Right now, Maxwell and I are headed to Corbin's house to see if they are still there.

My entire body is sore. After my medication wore off,

the pain set in everywhere. My muscles ache, my head pounds every time I have a thought, let alone move it, and my every breath burns up my throat. I can't move without hissing. I can't think without wincing. I don't know how I'm going to be any use saving Liesel, but I'm going to try and hope that Maxwell is truly on my side this time.

I glance over at Maxwell, who is driving in the seat next to me. He saved me when he could have just let me bleed to death. He brought me to Liesel when he didn't have to. It seems that for some reason, he's on my side, but that doesn't mean I don't have questions for him.

"Why does Corbin blame Liesel? Why not just her father?" I ask.

Maxwell's jaw ticks, and I know he doesn't want to answer. He starts to open his mouth, though, and I hold my breath.

"Corbin—"

My phone buzzes in the cupholder of our rental car, interrupting what Maxwell was going to say. Liesel's name flashes on the screen.

I grab it and press answer before the second ring.

"Hello," I say with a shaky voice.

"Langston? You're alive," her voice trembles, and I can hear her sniffles through the phone.

"I'm fine, huntress, thanks to you. You're always saving me."

She sobs a sigh of relief.

My heart clenches hearing her cry.

"Huntress, stop crying. I'm okay. Are you okay? Did Corbin hurt you?"

"No, he didn't hurt me. I'm fine."

"Where are you?"

That question she doesn't answer.

Maxwell studies me carefully; his ear perked as he tries to listen. *We are on the same side*, I remind myself. He can listen.

"Tell me, Liesel. I'll come to rescue you this moment. We can get Declan back without his help."

"You know about Declan? Do you know that my father is alive?"

"Yes, Maxwell told me."

Her voice strengthens. "You have to stay with the kids. You have to keep them safe. If my father finds out about them, he'll take them away from us or kill them. You have to protect them. Promise me."

Fuck, I don't want to promise her anything that I might break. I might not be with the kids in person, but I do know they are as safe as it gets.

"I promise to keep them safe," I say, hoping she doesn't realize my omission.

"Thank you," she sighs. "Can you put one of them on? I miss them."

Shit.

I glance at the time. It's after nine at night at my beach house. "Sorry, they're asleep."

"Oh, right. Of course, they're asleep. How is everyone doing? How are you feeling?"

"Everyone is good. I'm good. Liesel, tell me why you called."

She hesitates as if she's deciding better of it.

"If I tell you, you have to promise me to stay there with the kids. You can't come. I've got this."

"I know you've got this. You're the strongest woman I know. Now, will you tell me so you can go rescue Declan?"

"Corbin had the final clue. I was able to put it together with my half of the letter to figure out the location."

"Where?" I ask too quickly.

"Well, that's the thing. I only have part of the information. I think you have the other half."

"Okay, I don't think there was much left on the letter that we haven't already used."

"Anything that might have a clue about Russia?"

"Russia?" I say out loud.

Maxwell's eyebrows jump.

"Yes. But we don't know where exactly. Moscow is a big city, and we don't know where to start."

"Moscow," I say, thinking about the note while letting Maxwell know where we are headed.

He nods and turns, driving us back toward the airport.

I read through the note in my head, trying to figure out anything that could help us.

"There were numbers written at the bottom—352. I don't know what it means, but hopefully, it helps."

"It does, thank you," Liesel says, not explaining more.

"So you're going to Moscow with Corbin then?"

"Yes, we have a deal. Don't worry; we are on the same side at the moment."

I frown, not liking that she's trusting Corbin. "Don't trust him. Do what you have to do, but don't trust Corbin."

The line is quiet.

"Promise me."

"I promise. You promise me that you are going to stay with the kids?"

"I promise," I lie.

We end the call.

I look to Maxwell. "We need to hurry and get to Moscow. If I know Liesel, they are already there. We are running out of time."

6

LIESEL

I WIPE MY EYES, still moist with the tears at hearing Langston's voice. I hadn't realized until now just how much I worried that he wouldn't survive.

"I have the info we need," I tell Corbin.

Corbin nods stiffly, cleaning his gun. "Do you think he'll follow us?"

"Yes."

"I figured. Maxwell thinks too fondly of you and couldn't just tell the bastard to stay the hell at home." Corbin stands suddenly and walks across the living room to me. "That complicates things. Langston can't be there. He's only going to make it harder for us to kill your father."

"I know."

"Then why did you tell him the actual location?"

"So I can save him."

Corbin squints his eyes, not understanding.

"Trust me. This is the only way to stop Langston and to keep him from coming after us."

"As long as we are on the same side and still have a deal, that's all that matters."

"We do."

"Then, let's go to Moscow."

————

We walk into our one-bedroom hotel room in the center of Moscow. We used our real names to travel first class and, when booking the hotel, purposefully booking a room with one bed.

"You sure this plan of yours is going to work? I'm pretty sure it's just going to get me killed once Langston thinks we are sleeping in the same bed," Corbin paces.

I smirk. "Well, if he doesn't come to try and rescue me tonight, you'll be sleeping on the floor."

He groans. "I haven't slept on the floor since I was a kid."

"Well, you might tonight, so you better hope Langston comes."

Corbin unpacks his computer.

"Any movement on his tracking device?" I ask. Corbin had Maxwell put a tracking device on Langston when he dropped him off.

"Not yet, which means he's probably in the air."

We both stare at the screen, waiting for Langston's dot to appear to tell us he's in Moscow. We order room service and go over our plan again while we wait.

"You sure this is going to work? I'm not sure you have it in you to hurt him," Corbin says.

I laugh. "After everything that Langston and I have done to each other, this is nothing. I fucking sucked your cock remember?"

His eyes darken, telling me he does, in fact, remember.

I swallow hard.

I fucked up.

He laughs at my reaction. "You're so easy to mess with."

My heart slows, but it just goes to show I still don't trust this man. And as Langston said, I probably shouldn't.

"Look." Corbin points to the screen. He sits in the desk chair looking at the screen, while I stand behind him, looking over his shoulder at the dot that just appeared.

"He's here," I say, my breath catching.

"He is. You sure about this?"

"Yes, will you stop asking me that? This is the only way to protect him."

"If you say so."

I roll my eyes, snatch the laptop, and bring it to the bed where I can watch Langston's every move. The dot spends several minutes at the airport before it starts moving again.

Come find me. Come find me, killer.

"Is he moving toward us?"

I stare at the screen as the dot moves.

"Yes."

"Good, I don't want to sleep on the floor."

"You're such a baby."

"And you are a twisted, dark soul."

We both stare at each other. I suspect there is something we aren't telling the other, but that will have to wait. I have a husband to deal with.

Husband—I still can't believe I married him. It was the best and worst decision of my life. But if I die being married to Langston, it will have been worth it.

"He's here," I say, not believing he found us that fast. "Did you tell Maxwell where we are?"

"No, I should have, though. Your boy's good."

"Now what?" I ask.

"Don't 'now what' me, this is your plan."

I close the laptop and jump up off the bed to go listen at the door. A few minutes later, I see Langston pacing outside my door. He doesn't enter. He doesn't say anything. Then, he presses a hand to the door, and I know he's decided not to come in. He's going to just watch and wait, then follow us to the next location.

"Fuck," I whisper.

"What?" Corbin whispers back.

"He's not going to come in," I whisper.

"Oh, yes, he is."

Corbin marches toward me. He swoops me in his arms and lands a kiss on my lips.

"Corbin! Get off me!" I scream between kisses. "Stop, Corbin!"

The door pops open, and Langston stands there with a gun in his hand.

"Shit," Corbin says under his breath as he uses me like a shield.

I roll my eyes and pop him hard in the nose, knocking Corbin unconscious with a thud as he falls to the floor. Corbin and I had planned on him faking his unconsciousness, but I'm pretty sure I just knocked him out for real. It serves him right for kissing me instead of just letting me fake it.

Langston takes me in his arms like I'm a fragile piece of glass he's afraid he's going to break.

"Are you okay? Did he hurt you?" His eyes search up and down my body as his fingers caress my cheek, looking for clues that Corbin hurt me.

"I'm fine." I tremble in his arms all the same. Feeling Langston's hands on me again drives me wild with hunger and need. It doesn't matter that every second we are in Moscow, so close to my father, we are in imminent danger. My body craves Langston.

Langston's lips crash down on mine, devouring me in stark contrast to how gentle his hands are still holding me.

Clearly, he feels the same way. Luckily, I can use both of our weaknesses to my advantage.

"I missed you," I say, grabbing his neck and tilting his head to deepen the kiss.

"If you wouldn't have sent me away, you wouldn't have had to miss me at all."

"If I didn't, you'd be dead."

I bite the bottom of his lip, drawing blood.

He pulls back.

Our eyes snap to the other's, daring each other.

Langston whistles, and Maxwell enters.

"Remove Corbin," Langston says to Maxwell.

Maxwell nods and then scoops Corbin up under his arms. "I'll have him in the room next door. Let me know if you need me."

I'm silent as Maxwell removes Corbin from the hotel room. I don't know if Corbin is conscious enough to take on Maxwell, but I hope he is. I don't have a plan for seducing Maxwell.

The door shuts, and I turn to Langston, glaring at him. "So you can trust Maxwell, but I can't trust Corbin?"

He frowns. "Maxwell is on our side."

"So is Corbin."

"He was trying to rape you. If I hadn't come, he would have."

"No, I had the situation under control. I knocked him unconscious. Corbin and I have a deal. When he awakes, he'll realize his mistake. You should go."

"Go?" Langston cocks his head at me like he can't believe his ears as I stomp toward the door.

"Yes, it's not safe for you here. You shouldn't have come."

Langston walks toward me. The prowl on his face shoots through my body. If I didn't already plan on seducing him, my insides would be melting for him.

But the fear of losing Langston is what keeps me firm in my plan.

Langston takes my lips in his again, kissing me sweetly so as to seduce me. To shut me up with comments about how it isn't safe.

I grab his neck, and I feel him wince. My eyes draw large. "Are you hurt?"

I remove my hand, but Langston catches it, putting it back on his neck.

"I feel better when you touch me."

I hold my hand gingerly on his neck. "What happened? What surgery did you require?"

Langston smiles down at me. "The surgery doesn't matter. The injuries don't matter. What matters is that I'm here because of you. You saved me, and now it's my turn to save you."

"We can't—" I gasp as he kisses down my neck. "You can't rescue me. I have to save Declan first."

He grabs the hem of my shirt and lifts it over my head before kissing me again.

"We will, but I'm not letting you put yourself in danger again. We do this together, not with Corbin."

My eyes heat. I try to push our conversation out of my head because we won't be facing the danger together. Langston won't be saving me. I'll be the one saving him.

7

LANGSTON

I TOLD her we'd do this together. We'd take down her father and rescue Declan together.

It was a lie.

I can't have her anywhere near her father. I can't go through what I went through last time we faced her father's men. I won't let her face a firing squad again. She has to be safe, so that's what I plan on doing. I'll get her the hell out of here and back to my island with the kids. Back to where I can keep her safe, while Maxwell and I meet with her father to end this.

You might think I need a big team with lots of men to approach her father, but sometimes sneaking in with as few people as possible is better than a full-on attack with a full team. The dozens of people he can see coming and protect against, but with one or two, it's harder to know my next move.

Tonight though, I'll be enjoying my wife before I send her on the first plane out of here. It might be the last time I ever fuck her, so I plan on making the most of it by giving her a night that neither of us will forget.

Her sultry eyes and luscious lips pull me toward her.

"I want to fuck you slow and sweet. Make love to you like a husband should."

She smirks. "I don't want you to make love to me. I want you to fuck me."

Jesus Christ, this woman is perfect. How did I ever manage to stay away from her? To hate her?

Because I wanted to avoid losing her at all costs.

I can't lose her.

She has to stay alive. That's all I care about.

Me—I know I'm as good as dead. I'm not invincible.

Our lips join once again, crashing hard as our tongues swell and sweep through each other's mouths like a tornado. I'm dizzy from the first kiss. I could blame it on the blood loss I endured, but it's because of her. Everything I ever feel is because of her.

I've wasted so much of my life not having her. The second my hands touch the smooth skin just above her hips, I grow frantic. I can't wait to have her.

I grab her jeans and yank; they slide down her hips without even unbuttoning them. She's lost weight. With everything we've been through, food has been the furthest thing from her mind. The anxiety and stress make it hard. I'll have to send her back with orders to Kai and Siren to put some weight back on her.

But that isn't what has my eyes transfixed. My eyes are glues to the still fresh knife wound over her stomach. She's applied a gauze bandage to cover the spot, but I still mourn what she lost. *Did we lose a child? Did she lose the ability to have more children?*

She unhooks her bra and slides her panties down her body while I watch, speechless, still lost in thought.

She smiles a seductive grin as she hooks her fingers into my jeans and jerks me to her, breaking me from my worried trance.

"Naked, now," she purrs.

I don't have time to undress. "I have a better idea."

I invade her space as I kiss her again, consuming her thoughts. That's my goal for tonight, for her to completely lower her inhibitions. For her to give herself to me. Let me make the decision that's best for all of us. She may think she's trying to do the right thing in saving me, but she doesn't realize the only way to save me is if she stays alive. I won't be truly alive if she's not breathing.

I back her up against the window behind her. She gasps as her ass hits the cool glass.

"I want to fuck you so everyone can see. I want everyone to know that you're mine."

I flip her around so her breasts are against the window, and her ass is pressed against my crotch.

"I'm tired of hiding." I suck her earlobe.

She gasps. Her hands splay across the glass as she pulls her bottom lip into her mouth.

I undo my pants and kiss her neck.

"I'm tired of pretending I hate you."

I slap her ass before I shove my pants down enough for my cock to spring free. It slides between her ass cheeks and then between her legs as I feel how wet she already is for me.

"The world should know how much I fucking love you."

My cock slams inside her.

"Langston," she pants.

"That you're mine."

I fuck in and out of her against the glass for the entire town to see. There is a world of people below going about their business on this chilled night. Snowflakes are starting to fall down on their heads. A few of them look up.

Liesel gasps. "Can they see me?"

"All they see is that you're mine," I growl into her ear.

She tilts her head back and moans as I hit deeper inside her.

The lights are dim in our room; there is no way they can see much if they look up at us, but the thought that they could turns her on even more.

"My dirty huntress."

I fuck her harder.

"I need—"

I move my hand around her front, finding her clit, knowing that's what she was begging for. She's so responsive that I've been afraid that as soon as I touch her clit she's going to explode. I wanted my cock inside her when that happened.

I stroke her once, and then she comes undone.

"Killer!" she shouts. It's probably not the best thing to scream in a hotel room in the middle of Moscow, but I don't care. I'll fight anyone who comes to our room for a chance for my girl to feel good and be free to scream how she wants.

I pump into her once more, chasing my own orgasm. As I do, I feel her growing weak in my arms. I catch her.

"Make love to me in bed?" she asks, still wanting more.

I smile at her, afraid if we get into bed, our night will end too soon. The drugs pumping through my body combined with her exhaustion will cause us to drift off to sleep as soon as I fuck her again. I can't have that yet. I need more.

I shake my head as I scoop her up in my arms.

I'm still dressed, so as I lean down to tangle our tongues together again, she fights my shirt off my body.

I carry her toward the bathroom. I need to have her on every surface in this hotel room—the desk, the sink, the shower, and then finally the bed.

She reads my thoughts as I bend her over the counter of the bathroom, and our eyes meet. She reaches behind her and yanks my jeans and underwear down until they are a pile on the floor.

"Fuck me, show me I'm yours."

I sink into her body once again, feeling at home as soon as her tight walls surround me.

Our eyes meet in the mirror before I kiss down her back.

"Mine," I growl as I thrust harder into her.

Her body quakes as I do. It doesn't matter how many times I've had her; every time feels incredible—like I'm experiencing the greatest pleasure for the first time. And every time we finish, I think I imagined how good it felt. Being with someone couldn't possibly feel that good. But being with Liesel isn't like being with anyone. Being with Liesel is the only way I know how to exist.

I show her that she's my entire world as I fuck her against the bathroom counter, fuck her in the shower with her in my arms and the water pouring down her back, devour her on the desk with her legs spread and my face buried between them as her wet hair drips on me.

When she comes for the fifth time, and I look into her lidded eyes, I know that I have to let her rest. I can't keep pushing her body any further.

It's then that I know we must fuck in the bed so that when her body hits her wall of exhaustion, she can fall asleep in my arms and wake up on the island with the kids.

If I succeed, Declan will be on his way before she even wakes up. I have to succeed because of all the times I've failed her.

"Come here," I say, grabbing her hand and pulling her off the desk. She falls forward into my arms, too weak to even stand.

She grins up at me. "You've made me weak in the knees."

"And you thought I wasn't romantic."

I fall back and yank her with me as we land on the bed.

She doesn't have the strength to be on top right now, so I flip us over, inching us closer to the top of the bed. My cock is already hard and pushing between her legs that she lets fall open for me. Her pussy is still drenched with our combined cum.

"Please," she begs as her eyes begin to flutter closed. She can't stand to keep them open any longer and yet can't not have me inside her again.

I glance at the clock on the nightstands. It's after three in the morning. No wonder she's so tired.

I slide inside her in one slow stroke. This time fucking her is going to be about rocking her to sleep.

"I'm never going to let you go," I whisper against her lips as I push inside her.

"I'm never going to want you to."

There's a sadness in her voice, though. One that says we have to let each other go. I refuse to believe or accept her words. I will not be letting her go. She's mine. And I will fight every day to keep her.

"I love—"

She doesn't let me finish. With renewed energy, she flips us over until she's on top, riding me with much more vigor than I thought she had. I let her take control because she's a beautiful sight riding on top of me. Her breasts bounce up and down, and her gorgeous eyes shine down on me.

Our fingers tangle together as she rides me faster and faster. Our breaths turn to pants, our voices turn to moans, our hearts flutter so fast that I'm afraid I'll have a heart attack. None of that stops us.

"Fuck, I love you!" she screams as her orgasm pulses her pussy, milking me until my own orgasm spills from my cock.

She collapses on top of me like I expect.

I stroke her back with one arm as the other is still gripped by hers.

Within seconds I hear her breathing slow, and she's drifting off to sleep. I consider moving her, so she's snuggled up against me instead of on top of me, but I'd rather have her draped over my body for as long as possible.

I close my eyes, relaxing even though I know I won't be able to sleep.

And then I feel the clink of metal around my wrist.

My eyes fly open, afraid that someone has infiltrated the room and Liesel is in danger. I fling her hard off my body to my side so I can use my body to protect her as best as I can.

I yank my arm, which is now handcuffed to the bed, but it doesn't break free. I try again, but the metal bed frame doesn't shift.

"Liesel, stay behind me. I won't let anyone hurt you."

I sit up, trying to push her behind me.

My eyes scan the room, but I don't see anyone.

"Who is it?" Liesel asks.

"I'm not sure. My gun—"

"Is in the bathroom with your jeans," she whispers.

"Don't!" I try to grab her, but she's already running toward the bathroom to retrieve my gun. I search the room, but I still can't spot who's in our room.

"Here," Liesel says from the other side of the bed. I reach out to grab the gun from her while keeping my eyes on the floor near my bed. I assume whoever is in our room is beneath the bed and trying to figure out how to shoot us before I shoot him.

Clink.

I never feel the gun in my hand. Instead, my other wrist is attached to the other side of the bed with another handcuff.

I look up at Liesel's big eyes as she stands naked before me.

"Liesel, what are you doing?" I ask, realizing that no one

47

else is in the room with us. It's just Liesel and me. She's the one who restrained me.

"I'm sorry," she says with tears in her eyes.

"What. Are. You. Doing?"

She doesn't answer me. Instead, she looks to the door.

It opens.

"Took you long enough," Corbin says as he enters.

"How did you…?" I say.

Corbin smirks at me. "Maxwell and I have been brothers for a long time. I know his weaknesses."

"You killed him?"

"No, I just made him see reason."

I frown and then yank on my cuffs, put on me by the woman I love.

"Excuse me," Liesel says suddenly and runs to the bathroom.

I hear her vomit.

Corbin looks as distressed as I am as we listen. For a moment, we both seem concerned about the girl in the bathroom. Me because I can't live without her. Corbin because he can't succeed on his mission if something happens to her.

A few minutes later, Liesel reemerges with a robe wrapped around her.

"Liesel? What's wrong?"

She shakes her head. "I've been a nervous wreck about doing this to you all day. I wish it didn't have to be this way."

"What way? Liesel, uncuff me. We have to fight your father together."

"No. Don't lie to me. Don't tell me you didn't have the same plan to drug me and send me back to the island where your friends would hold me captive."

"Huntress, you can't kill; you need my help."

"I'm sorry."

Then she nods at Corbin, who I realize is here to do the thing she can't.

I don't look away as Corbin approaches and places the needle into my neck.

A single tear rolls down her cheek as the drugs take hold of me, knocking me slowly unconscious.

I fight the drugs as long as I can.

"I'm sorry, killer, but I have to protect you. I love you too much to risk losing you."

And then I succumb to the darkness once again.

8

LIESEL

LANGSTON DRIFTS OFF, and then Corbin checks his pulse, but I can tell from here that he's still breathing. The sedative Corbin gave him shouldn't hurt him.

"You okay?" Corbin asks.

I nod. "Just a little queasy."

"I wasn't talking about that." He hesitates, running his hand through his hair. "This is for the best. If Langston steps one foot inside your father's club, then he's a dead man. If you want Langston to live, this is the only way."

"I know." I grip the edges of the robe, tightening it around my body. My eyes peer up at Corbin in a shy way.

"Get dressed. I'll be right outside when you're ready." Corbin walks out of the hotel room, leaving me alone with a sleeping Langston.

The tears start falling freely now. I'm not sure if this will be the last time I ever see him. I'm going to face my father to do whatever it takes to get Declan back, so it very well could be.

I wipe my tears and then quickly shower and get dressed. I pull my hair up in a high ponytail after quickly blow-drying it. I know I'm just stalling, taking as much time as I possibly can to prolong the goodbye.

Langston is already unconscious, so the goodbye should be easy. But for some reason, I linger in the bedroom, feeling so deep in my bones that I have to make this goodbye count. I have to pull every bit of joy I can from this moment because this goodbye is going to be our last.

No, don't think that way. I'm going to go kill my father, get Declan back, and I'll be back with Langston on the island in a couple of days. This isn't goodbye.

I lean over a motionless Langston and kiss his lips. "This isn't goodbye."

I can feel the tears welling again. I have to leave before I change my mind and stay.

"I love you."

And then I walk out the door.

Corbin is leaning against the wall. He looks up when I exit.

"Ready?" he asks.

I nod. "He's going to be okay, right?"

Corbin walks toward me. He puts my head in the palms of his hands, cupping my face gently. "You're doing the right thing. The drugs will wear off in twenty-four hours. Maxwell's will wear off a couple of hours earlier, and I've given him strict instructions to get Langston out of here. With any luck, we will have already killed your father by then."

"Where is Maxwell?"

"In the hotel room one over. I have cameras on both rooms." Corbin pulls up his phone to show me the feed. "If they wake up early, we'll know."

"Let's go."

I pull out of Corbin's grasp and walk downstairs to the taxi waiting for us.

We climb in and don't speak on the way to my father's club. There is nothing left to say. We have a plan, and we are going to do it. For now, we fight on the same side. We both want my father dead.

The car stops, and we climb out.

Snow is still falling as we enter the single unsuspecting door that leads to the unnamed club.

There is a guard at the door who scans us with a metal detector.

Corbin offered me a gun, but I knew I'd never get it in. My scan is clean. The man turns to do Corbin's scan, but before he can, Corbin removes his gun and two knives and hands them to the security guard.

The man looks from me to Corbin. "Mr. Dunn has been expecting you. I'll show you to a room where you can wait for him."

My heart rate spikes, but I don't let it show. I don't know how my father was expecting me to show up tonight, but it seems that he has eyes and ears everywhere.

Corbin tries to take my hand as we follow the guard, but I swat his hand away. I don't need any help, and I don't want him to try to give me strength—I've got this.

The guard opens a door after we've walked down two sets of stairs and turned at least a half dozen times through various hallways. Wherever he's taking us, it's deep underground and not going to be easy to escape from.

He motions for us to step inside, so we do.

My eyes widen at the number of people in the room. More than a dozen men stand with guns strapped across their chests like we are the most dangerous terrorists they have ever met.

The man slams the door shut behind us. Suddenly, I'm back with Langston facing the firing squad. Except for this time, I'm with a man who is still more or less my enemy, even though we are facing a greater enemy.

I scan the room, looking for my father, but I don't see any man old enough to be him, nor do I see any man who appears to be in charge. They are all wearing the same bland outfit of camouflage plants and a dark shirt meant to look menacing.

"Coward!" I yell, knowing my father must be listening. How cowardly of him to have his men kill us without even facing us.

Corbin grabs my hand again. "I'm sorry." He knows we've failed. This is how it ends. Our plan failed.

I shake my head and release Corbin's hand. I refuse to go down like this. This is not how my life ends. I know my fate, and this isn't it.

"You've been hiding from me my entire life! If you're going to kill me, at least be man enough to do it face to face. Don't send your men in to do your dirty work for you," I say, looking into the camera in the corner of the room I guarantee my father is watching.

The room is silent after my outburst. None of the men train their guns on Corbin or me. Maybe I was wrong or a bit overdramatic to immediately think we were about to die.

We both wait.

And wait.

And wait.

We wait so long that Corbin and I end up sitting back to back in the center of the room, resting our backs on each other because there isn't anywhere else for us to sit.

Finally, a door opens, and a man in a suit enters. He has peppered hair and my eyes. I know instantly he's my father.

"Thanks for waiting. I don't do business before six in the morning," he says with a smirk.

Corbin and I both jump to our feet. I immediately feel the

urge to attack him, so I start running toward him without thinking. Luckily, Corbin grabs my arms and holds me back.

"I take it you didn't enjoy waiting."

"I've waited my entire life for this. I can wait a few hours," I growl back.

"Well, let's begin," my father says, snapping his fingers.

His men start rearranging the room, bringing in a circular table, three chairs, a bottle of whiskey, glasses, and a tray of cigars.

"Please, have a seat." My father motions for us to take our seats.

Corbin and I sit across from my father. I don't know what game he's playing, but whatever it is, I'm ready. He doesn't realize how strong I am, how much pain I can endure. When you lose a child, nothing affects you anymore.

My father smiles at Corbin. "It's good to see you again, Corbin. I'm glad she brought you instead of that schmuck she's married to."

Corbin stares my father down. I'm happy to see for a fact that Corbin is on my side in this.

"Why?" I ask, knowing it's the only question I care to know before I kill this man.

"Why? I built an empire. One grander than the one your husband belongs to. Mine is more secretive, more danger-ous. It has made me a very wealthy man. I had plans to pass it on to my son, but then I had a daughter. Your mother wasn't strong enough to have another. So I looked else-where. It turns out, I took an injury to the groin that left it impossible for me to have kids either. That left you as my only option." He snorts, laughing at the ridiculous idea of depending on little, pathetic me.

He's right. It is ridiculous. If I took over his empire, I'd just purposefully burn it to the ground.

"You're weak, just like your mother. I knew it from the

moment I laid eyes on you and watched you play with the boy across the street. I knew who he'd grow up to be—our enemy. And I knew you wouldn't see it that way. So I ensured he stayed away, that he hated you. But I should have killed the bastard when he was a kid."

I want to jump out of my chair and attack my father, but Corbin slips a hand onto my thigh, steadying me. I know I'll have an opportunity to kill this man; I just need to bide my time.

"And then you got pregnant."

"I didn't get pregnant like a horny teenager who didn't know how to use a condom. I was raped."

"I know. I was thankful that the father of your children wouldn't be that boy from across the street. Your children would still be of the blood of my enemy, though."

Our eyes lock in a battle. *I'm going to kill you*, my eyes say. *I already destroyed you*, his eyes say in return.

"So I had Corbin take your son so I could raise him and prepare him to take over my empire."

"Where is Declan?" I ask.

My father smiles. "He's safe. He's already turning into quite the young boy. I have every confidence that he's strong enough to take my place."

"That's because you brainwashed him."

"No, it's because he's strong."

"Why send me the note? Why fake your death? Why have me seek out my son?"

"That's the question, isn't it?"

I frown. He's not going to tell me.

"What do you want from me? I'll give you whatever you want. You want money; I'll give you money. You want my body; you can have it. You want my soul; it's yours. You want to watch me burn; I'll tie myself to the stake. Just release my son."

"But you haven't played the final game yet. I can't just give you Declan. You have to earn him. And since you brought Corbin instead of your husband, I'll let you play."

I stiffen in my seat. All of my rage floods my heart. I'm ready to play whatever stupid game he has planned. I wasn't bluffing earlier; I'll do whatever it takes to get him back.

"I'm putting my money on you losing, though. You can't get Declan back while you still love that man. Love is weak. You're weak. And soon, you're going to realize it too."

9

LANGSTON

I OPEN MY EYES, but I wish I was still asleep. My head is pounding, my mouth is dryer than a desert, and the light in the room is irritating my eyes.

And then I remember.

"Liesel!" I yell. I try to jump up, but my arms are still tied to the bed.

"Woah, easy there. You don't want to cause more damage," Maxwell says.

I stare at him.

"Where is she? What happened?"

"I presume she's fine, and she's with Corbin going after her father. After I dragged Corbin's lifeless body out of this room and into mine, he attacked me. I'm strong, but Corbin has always been the better fighter. Plus, he had the element of surprise. He knocked me out, tied me to the bed, and drugged me. I woke up about an hour ago."

"You've been awake for an hour? Does that mean you know where they went? Did they go to the address?"

"I know where they went."

"Untie me, let's go." I yank on my wrists, the metal

cutting through my skin. The pain barely registers. Liesel went after her father. She's in danger. I have to help her.

"No."

"What do you mean, no? Untie me! That's why we came here, to go after Liesel. To keep her safe."

Maxwell frowns. "We also came here to rescue Declan."

I know he's right. "We can get him after we get Liesel out of here."

"Can we? Do you really think two men sneaking into his lair is going to end well? He's had years to prepare for this moment. He's got dozens of men, security systems, a plan."

"We can do it. We can defeat him."

Maxwell looks me in the eyes like he's trying to understand something. "Do you think Liesel isn't strong enough to get Declan back? To kill her father?"

"She's strong enough."

"Then why not do this with her? Why send her home?"

"Because I can't risk losing her."

Maxwell pauses for a beat, understanding washing over him. He looks at me with a sadness that says he never wants to fall in love. In his eyes, love makes you weak. He doesn't realize the truth is the opposite. Love makes you incredibly strong. But losing that love—that's the only weakness.

"I'll untie you."

Maxwell walks over to the corner of the bed and begins to work on unlocking the handcuff. I could get out of the handcuffs, but it would take me a lot longer, and I'd fuck up my shoulder to do it, so I'm thankful for Maxwell's help.

Five minutes later, he has both of the handcuffs off my wrists.

He tosses clothes at me.

"Get dressed, and then we can go."

"You're still going to help me go after Liesel?"

There's a pause. "Yes."

I pull on my jeans then have my arms pushing through my shirt. "Did they go to the club?"

"Yes, but then they moved to another location. I have the address, and our rental car is waiting. Let's go."

My heart thumps wildly. I'm terrified of what we are going to find, but I have to help Liesel. Maxwell is right that if she's already with her father, it's going to be hard to get her to leave. That doesn't mean I won't try.

Most of all, I will do everything I can to ensure she lives.

10

LIESEL

I'm so sick of games. I'd rather just fight this out. Let's all pull our guns out and duel rather than go through another game. I'm tired, and I want this over. My exhaustion is multiplied by the pressure—I have to win. That's my only purpose in this world—to be my kid's protector, not their mother. I save them; I just don't get to love them.

If my father wants to play more games, then let's play. I never lose a game.

"If I win the game, I get Declan?" I ask, needing to understand the terms. I can't trust my father, but I at least have to know that winning will give me a shot at getting my son back.

"No. If you win, then you take his place. You become the heir to my empire, and he goes free to live with whomever you want," my father replies.

I suck in a breath. This is the second time a man has wanted to take my life in exchange for freeing my son. I now owe my life to both Corbin and my father. It doesn't matter, though. They don't realize it isn't a good trade; my life isn't worth much.

"Let's play," I say.

"Igor, please bring out the game," my father speaks to one of the men I forgot were in the room. My eyes roam around the room to the still-standing guards with guns strapped to their chests. Not only do I have to convince my father, but I have to convince these men to let my son go.

It hits me all at once—why my father sent me the note, why he's using my son as bait, why he wants to play these games. He doesn't think Declan is cut out to be his heir. He's manipulating me into becoming what he wants. His games are meant to brainwash me into being the monster he is.

So I'll show him how evil of a monster I can be. He'll see I truly am the devil's daughter. It's the only chance I have of winning.

Igor brings a box out and sets it on the table.

Corbin and I eye the box carefully. I don't know how helpful Corbin is going to be, but bringing him as a backup was better than Langston. If Langston were here, these men would be shooting at us.

My father opens the box and pulls out a board before handing me a bag of my game pieces.

"Chess?" I ask dubiously.

"Chess will test your mental strength and strategy."

I open the bag and find that I have the white pieces, while my father has black. I've never played chess before, so I'm not holding my breath at being very good.

"I beat you at chess, and Declan goes free?"

My father snickers. "No, you beat me at chess while completing tasks that test your physical and emotional strength, then Declan goes free. Every time one of us captures a piece, you must complete a task to continue the game."

"And Corbin?"

"He can help you. You need to learn to rely on a man who

can actually assist you, instead of a man who works for Enzo Black and could betray you at any moment."

"Actually, Langston used to work for Kai Black, not Enzo. And he quit."

"We all know Enzo is the real leader of that empire, not his wife."

I laugh. "You have no idea what you're talking about."

"Prove me wrong. Prove that a woman is strong enough for a life like this."

I don't know exactly what my father does, but I can guess. He sells drugs, weapons, women—anything that can make him money. It's a life I've always been running from, but it seems like my destiny.

"Who goes first?" I ask.

My father smiles. "White always goes first. Do I need to tell you the rules?"

"No, I'm a fast learner." I know enough, and the rest I'll learn. It's not really about the game of chess anyway. It's about the tests he's about to make me endure. He wants me to win. He needs me to win. But he needs me to prove I'm strong enough first. When it comes down to it, if I succeed in his tasks, then he'll forfeit the game to me.

I move one of my center pawns two steps forward.

"Good, I was afraid you had no idea how to play the game." My father counters with one of his own pawns.

The only experience I have with chess is from watching a movie once. They played the opening sequence, and so I start by trying to mirror it and get a feel for how each piece moves.

I move my knight next.

So does my father.

I move another knight.

My father moves a bishop.

I move a bishop.

He moves another pawn.

I move another bishop.

We both castle.

We've developed our pieces—moved them into strategic places in the center of the board. It feels like a dance, moving our pieces together without attacking. In the movie I watched, the game cut away at this point, so I don't know how to move next.

My eyes cut to Corbin out of the corner of my vision. He's studying the board carefully. I don't want to ask him for help so soon, but if he has any idea how to play the game, I'll take any help I can get.

On the other hand, this isn't about winning the chess game. It's about being willing to complete any task, sacrifice anything, show him I'm strong enough to do what needs to be done to run his empire.

Now isn't the time to ask Corbin for help.

I move my pawn clearly into a spot where it can be captured.

My father grins, taking my pawn.

One of his men walks over and hands him a folder. My father nods and opens the folder. He slides the contents across the table to me.

Corbin strains his head to read the papers as I pull them toward me.

Divorce papers.

"You know if I sign these, it doesn't mean I'm divorced? Langston also has to sign, and a judge has to agree. This takes time."

"I understand how filing for divorce usually works. In your case, let's just say the divorce will be approved at an expedited speed."

I run my thumb across the ring on my finger. It's not giving Langston up exactly. Being divorced doesn't mean that we've stopped loving each other. When this is all over, we could get remarried. This is an easy sacrifice to make.

"Hand me a pen," I say firmly, showing no emotion. Signing some divorce papers means nothing to me.

My father slides me a fancy pen with engraving on the side. I turn the pen open and sign my name across the bottom line. Then I slide the papers back, raising an eyebrow in defiance of my father's weak test.

Then my father signs the other side of the document where Langston is supposed to sign.

I admit that I can't fully hide my emotions seeing my father so easily dissolve my marriage.

His man returns to take the papers and leave the room, while my father pulls his cell from his pocket. "Judge Hider, it's Dunn. I have a divorce I need your sign-off on ASAP." My father hangs up before the person on the other end can reply.

It doesn't mean anything. It's just a piece of paper. It won't stop me from loving Langston.

I follow my father's gaze to my hand on the table, and I realize I'm fidgeting with my wedding ring.

I pull my hand into my lap.

"Now that you will no longer be married within a matter of hours, take off your wedding ring. I'm sure I can get you a good price for it."

My father's gaze is a challenging one. He expects me to protest, put up a fight, and force him to have one of his men physically remove the ring from my finger. He doesn't know that by taking a physical object from me, he's taking nothing. This piece of metal on my finger is meaningless. It doesn't make my heart stop loving Langston.

I slide the ring off my finger and place it on the table between us.

"Good girl," he says.

I wince inside, hating being treated like a dog.

"Now that you're one step closer to being free of that man let's continue."

It's my move, but I understand the game a bit more now. I understand what game my father is truly playing.

I move a pawn.

He does too.

We continue to move pieces back and forth before I finally have an opportunity to take one of his pawns.

Igor walks back over with a laptop in his hand and gives it to my father.

"Every time any piece is captured, you have to complete a task or forfeit the game." He slides the laptop in front of me. "This task should be relatively painless. Transfer any money in your bank accounts to me. All of your assets will be mine."

I quickly make the transfers and then slide the laptop back to my father.

"Satisfied?" I ask.

"Well, you've proven that you can follow orders and make sacrifices, but there's more to being me than that."

"You mean like being an ass who abandons his daughter to go kill people?"

He shakes his head. "Play."

He moves a piece, then I do, and he captures one of my knights.

Fuck, I didn't even see that move.

Igor comes over, not carrying anything this time, which somehow scares me more. Before, it was about paperwork, now it's about to get physical—I can feel it.

My father whispers something in his ear. Igor nods and then steps to the side of my father.

"You've endured emotional suffering, but now it's time to see if you can endure physical pain." By the coy smile on his face, I already know what he's about to say. It doesn't terrify me at all.

"There's nothing quite like the sting of a bullet as it pierces your skin."

"Really? Are you going to shoot your own daughter? How does that prove anything? How does it prove how strong she is? If you want to know how strong she is, just ask, I've seen her endure plenty of physical pain. She stab—" Corbin says.

"It's okay, Corbin. If my father wants to shoot me, then let him shoot me. I couldn't possibly hate him more than I already do, and I would enjoy using it as added motivation when I eventually kill him," I say.

My father lights a cigar and then leans back in his chair as he puffs on it. "I won't be the one shooting you."

"What?"

"Igor will shoot you."

"Coward."

He shrugs. "I don't get my hands dirty for anyone who isn't worth it. So far, you haven't proved your worth."

Somehow, the fact that he isn't going to be the one to shoot me pisses me off even more.

I move to stand; I won't cower in front of this man. Corbin grabs my arm.

"Shoot me instead," Corbin says, holding me in my chair as he looks to my father.

My father takes the cigar out of his mouth, and Corbin continues. "Liesel and I are on the same team; shoot me instead."

My father snickers. "So you got two men to fall in love with you. Is your pussy that good?"

I spit in his face. I don't care that he's my father. I don't care that he has my son; I can't believe he spoke to me like that.

"There's that fire. I knew you'd eventually fight back. But only her husband could take a bullet for her."

"Marry me then first," Corbin says.

I wasn't sure if Corbin was on my side, but I'm sure now. He's willing to do anything to keep me from getting shot, including taking the bullet himself and marrying me.

Maybe he's after my father's empire, and taking a bullet for me seems like his best shot? It doesn't matter because I'm only going to let Corbin help when it's absolutely necessary. I can take being shot.

"No," I say before my father can speak. "I'll take the bullet. This is my fight." I turn to my father. "But Corbin is the man I brought here. I just signed the divorce papers for my marriage to Langston. For all intents and purposes, Corbin and I are married. We are a team, and you are going to accept that."

My father dusts off the end of his cigar into a dish. "I'll accept your terms. Igor, shoot whichever one of them they decide."

"Me," I say, pushing Corbin back into his chair.

"But—" I can see the pain in his eyes. *Maybe he does care about me more than I thought? Or maybe it's because he knows my secret and is afraid of what will happen?* He's never spoken the truth of the secret to me, but I suspect he already knows. However, he can't speak it out loud, or my father will know, and that would change everything.

"I'm fine. I need to do this." I need to prove to my father that I'm strong enough. I'll only let Corbin help when I can't do the task. This one I can do.

Reluctantly, Corbin lets go of my arm.

I stand. "Where do you want me?"

"Where you're standing is fine," Igor answers.

I notice that the men behind me have moved out of the way.

I hold my arms out casually to the side, unsure of where he's going to shoot me or what's going to happen afterward. Am I going to get any medical assistance? I doubt it. I doubt I'll get any painkillers either, another reason I should take the bullet instead of Corbin. I need Corbin's muscle, his ability to fight and shoot. I don't need him physically impaired. I'm not much of a shot, so getting shot myself won't matter.

I don't say anything as Igor takes his time readying his gun. My instinct is to close my eyes to keep from flinching, but I refuse to show that I'm scared.

I won't show fear.

I won't show pain.

I'm a rock. I'll do anything for my kids. This is just another step to prove it.

And then his gun is aimed at me. I'm not good enough with a gun to understand exactly where he's aiming.

Without warning, he fires.

I blink, the only reaction I allow myself.

At first, I feel nothing. I'm guessing with how close he shot me and how quickly the bullet sped through my body that it stopped the pain. I don't even know where he shot me.

Suddenly, I feel the damage.

The middle of my thigh. I'm surprised I haven't fallen to the ground or doubled over from the pain.

Screamed.

Cried.

Succumbed.

The pain hits me again and again in waves crashing through me. It started in my leg but quickly spread everywhere.

I feel my father's eyes on me, and I refuse to give in. I will not let any pain show in my appearance.

I'm not sure if I can really walk on it, but I take a step all the same. When I put my foot down, I realize that bearing weight on it isn't a good idea. Instead, I hop on my left leg back toward my chair.

Corbin can't stand it and jumps up, putting my arm over his shoulders.

I open my mouth to speak.

"If you protest me helping you right now, I'm going to drag you out of here right now."

I shut my mouth and let Corbin help me to my seat.

I continue to glare at my father.

I'm going to kill him.

Me.

Not Corbin.

Me.

"Can you get me a first aid kit?" Corbin asks Igor.

"No," my father says.

"Really? Do you want her bleeding all over your chair and carpet? That's going to be a bitch to clean," Corbin tries again.

My father frowns as he sucks on his cigar and then lifts a glass of whiskey to his lips in his other hand.

"I'm not going to give her any medications, just something to keep the blood off your floors and her conscious enough to finish this game," Corbin pleads.

I take deep, steadying breaths as I stare down at my father. I don't care if he lets Corbin tend to my wound. I don't care if I bleed out on the floor right here. All I care about is saving Declan and ensuring this man dies.

My life doesn't matter; I will succeed either way.

11

LANGSTON

MAXWELL STOPS the car in the middle of a field, and my heart sinks. I know before I step out of the car that Liesel isn't here. That doesn't stop me from jumping out of the car and running through the field, yelling her name over and over.

Birds squawk as I run.

The wind howls.

The thick brush stabs into my leg through my jeans as I run, searching for any sign of Liesel, Corbin, or her father.

I find nothing.

And yet, I keep running.

I need to have hope that she's here. I need to have hope that I can do something to help her, to protect her after all the times I've failed.

I search every place as far as I can see, but this place looks untouched by people.

Maxwell said he tracked her cell here. *Does that mean...?*

My heart sinks.

Is she dead? Is she buried out here?

I turn and get a good look at Maxwell, who is leaning against the outside of the car, waiting.

He's not searching.

He's not frantic to find his brother.

He knows he isn't here.

Fuck.

He tricked me.

I thought I could trust him.

I thought we were on the same side, but of course, he's still loyal to his brother.

I stomp back toward him calmly, trying to settle my anger and focus it on how to find Liesel. That should be my focus, not this asshole.

But I can't let his action go completely unnoticed.

"Didn't find her?" he asks.

My jaw ticks, but I don't answer.

"I've been looking at a map, and there looks to be a small town a couple of miles from here. I think we should search—"

I hit him square in the jaw, shutting him up.

I intend to only hit him one time. Getting into a scuffle with him won't help anything.

"What was that for?"

I turn, glaring at him. "You brought me to the middle of nowhere knowing Liesel isn't here. Where. Is. She?"

Maxwell's facade drops. He looks away for a moment, unable to hide his guilt.

I don't have time for his apologies.

I march over to the driver's seat and throw the door open.

As I'm climbing inside, Maxwell grabs my arm and throws a punch.

I duck just before his fist can land on my eye. Then, I wrap my arms around his waist and tackle him to the ground.

I throw another punch, hitting him hard in the head.

He punches me in my gut until I'm gasping for air.

I fall back as he punches, but I have too much rage to let him get the upper hand, even for a second.

I throw another punch.

Then another.

And another.

I no longer remember who I'm fighting. In my vision, Maxwell morphs into Liesel's father.

I'm going to kill him; nothing will stop me.

"Put your hands where we can see them," a deep voice says.

Those words break me from my spell.

I release Maxwell, and we both carefully put our hands in the air as a dozen armed men approach us.

I look over at Maxwell out of the corner of my eye and see his eyes dilated. This wasn't part of his plan. He brought me here to get me away from Liesel.

I smirk because I know these men will take me to her. I'd rather be in chains, facing death near Liesel than safely away from her.

12

LIESEL

I FEEL the pressure in my thigh with every breath. Corbin wrapped gauze and a bandage tightly around my leg to stop the bleeding, but that was all he was allowed to do. Blood-stains cover my jeans and the carpet below. Pain radiates through my body like a stampede of horses.

How can a bullet wound in my leg affect my ability to breathe? For some reason, my chest feels tight.

I'm dying.

I have no doubt about that, but then again, I've always been dying—slowly, torturously. It's why I should have never had kids, never married, never fallen in love.

I'm dying faster than I first thought. The wound in my leg has quickened the death I knew was to come.

I can't stop myself from dying, but I can ensure those I love are safe before I die—that I vow. I will not allow myself to die until my father is dead. Until my kids are safe. Until Langston is safe.

"It's your move," I say to my father, now on his second cigar and third glass of whiskey.

"You look pale. Are you sure you don't need a break?" He puffs smoke directly in my face.

"Move," I say, gritting my teeth to keep from jumping across the table and strangling him.

Corbin shifts uncomfortably in his seat next to me. He wants this to end as badly as I do, kill my father just like I do. He, too, knows my time is limited. If I'm going to kill my father before I take my last breath, then I need this to move faster.

My father takes his sweet time moving a piece. He studies the entire board like he hasn't already decided on his move. Finally, he moves a bishop into the center of the board, seeming to sacrifice it, but I can't see why.

My head is spinning. My eyes are glossy. I'm not going to be able to think clearly when it comes to the game.

I don't know what my father has planned next, but if it's physical torture, anything could finish me off. I'm not sure I should be sacrificing or taking any chess pieces that aren't absolutely necessary for me to win.

I reach my hand forward, but it shakes.

Corbin grabs it and gives it a squeeze next to me, reminding me he's on my side.

"What do you think?" I say quietly. I'm sure my father will see me asking for help as a weakness, but I don't have a choice. My choice is to lose on my own or ask for help and win.

Corbin takes my knight and moves it forward. I have no idea what he's doing, but at least we didn't capture any pieces, so I don't have to do any challenges to keep playing the game.

Corbin stands up, releasing my hand. *Why is he letting go of my hand? Doesn't he know that holding his hand is the one thing keeping me alive?*

My father once again takes his sweet time moving. Not

because he's not an expert at this game, but simply because taking his time draws me closer to death.

Corbin sinks back down into his chair next to me, and then he shoves something else into my hand. It's cold and wet.

I glance down. A glass of water rests in my hand.

It takes all of my focus to lift it to my lips, but as the cold liquid slips past my lips and down my throat, I realize how life-giving water is. The small glass of water ensures that I'll live for another hour instead of dropping dead shortly.

My father moves, and I have no choice now but to take one of his pieces, but I glance to Corbin out of the corner of my eye to see if he agrees.

He gives me a tight nod.

I move my queen, taking one of his bishops.

Fearlessly, I stare at my father. I'm not afraid. Do your worst. Death doesn't scare me.

My father must think that I'm not capable of standing. Instead of forcing me to do something physical, he goes for my heart. He slides some papers to me.

Three papers, to be exact.

As soon as I see Rose's name, I know what these are.

It doesn't matter. Soon they won't belong to me anyway. Soon they will be safe with Langston. Signing over my rights as a mother is meaningless. A piece of paper doesn't make me a mother any more than a piece of paper stops me from being a mother. I've never truly been their mother, just their protectors. Phoenix has always been their mother, and Langston, their father. It doesn't matter that neither of them gave their blood to my kids; they loved them all the same.

I quickly glance at the papers. They don't give my kids to anyone, just relinquish my rights.

From my father's smug expression, he doesn't think I'll

do this. He thinks this will be the thing that breaks me, the thing that ruins me.

"Give up. Surrender, and you'll live, my daughter. You'll get medical treatment just as soon as you lose. You can go back to living with your two children, but I keep your third to raise as my heir. Give up, and you still have a chance to be happy."

He doesn't know I'll die either way. And I refuse to know any one of my children isn't safe.

"Pen," I demand.

He picks up a pen and slides it to me. His eyes narrow slightly as I take the pen.

I have no time to waste. Every second I stall is a second closer to death.

I sign all three quickly, somehow managing to not let my hand shake. Then I shove the papers hard across the table.

"Your move," I say.

My father's eyes widen. Instead of puffing on his cigar, he puts it out. He sits straighter in his chair. For the first time, he seems proud of me. Of course, a man who gave up his only daughter would think me signing away my children makes me strong.

He moves faster this time.

I move.

He moves.

Again, I'm forced to take another piece. He sees it, I see it. Actually, I see a way I can win, but I'm going to have to take two pieces and sacrifice another to do it.

I can tell by the gleam in his eye that he sees my path to victory too. He won't let me win this game easily. He still may not let me win at all. And surviving three more challenges is not a given.

Three.

More.

And then Declan is mine.

Then I can fight back.

Then I can find the perfect time to kill my father.

I gather all my strength as I take his rook.

His eyes shine brighter, prouder.

"The next challenge is simple. Prove that you don't love Langston. Prove that your heart is open to being with another man."

I frown, guessing where he's going with this, and it makes my already uneasy stomach twist on itself.

"You want me to fuck someone who isn't Langston?"

My father laughs in my face. "Why would I want you to do something that could just result in you having more bastards? You have plenty of those already."

I frown. "Don't talk about my children that way."

"Except they aren't your children anymore. They aren't your anything."

His words don't have the effect he intended them to. Instead, I smile at him like I have a secret he will never know. I've already won. Keeping my kids safe is all that matters, not my legal parental rights.

"You're going to have to be more explicit with what you want from me."

"People forgive their spouses fucking another all the time. Fucking a man won't prove that you stopped loving Langston. Kissing another man. Letting him touch you in an intimate way while his lips are pressed against yours. That is much harder to forgive."

Why is he talking about forgiveness?

"Who will I be kissing?"

My father looks to my left. Corbin.

I look at him, and he has a pained expression on his face. I've sucked his cock. We've threatened to kill each other. And yet, kissing him does seem harder than fucking him. I don't understand why, but somehow my father has realized this truth.

I don't have a choice, and neither does Corbin. He has to kiss me. I have to let him. And I have to prove that I'm enjoying the kiss, giving part of myself over while Corbin's lips are pressed against mine. I have to open my heart during the kiss and encourage Corbin's hands to wander over my body like I'm his.

I stand, deciding that I need it for courage. Standing will make me more lightheaded and more likely to lean on Corbin, making it seem like I'm falling just a bit for him.

Corbin stands wordlessly next to me. I know he's in this just as much as I am. He's just as willing to do whatever it takes to win, same as me.

I don't let myself think.

I don't let my father win.

I lean in and let my lips brush against Corbin's while I open my heart and let it bleed.

13

LANGSTON

My arms are tied behind my back, as are Maxwell's behind me.

We've been led into a small, dark room. I assume it's our prison until they decide they have a need for us, but I sense Liesel is close. If she's here, Maxwell and I will escape. We'll find her; we have to.

I'm sure the men who led us into this room think keeping the lights off will dull my senses, and I'll be less of a threat. They don't know I thrive in the darkness. I can see better here than in the light.

I'm not sure about Maxwell, so I can't signal to him the moment we should fight back. I'm sure he'll catch on, though. If not, I have no problem taking down the six guards in the small room with us.

I hear the thud of the door, locking us inside with our enemies. This is the moment to attack.

Before I can spring into action, a bright light draws my attention. A screen has been turned on in the center of the room.

On the screen, Liesel is standing in the center of a room, face to face with Corbin.

I should scan the room behind her to figure out where she might be. I need to figure out what danger she's in and how to save her, but all I can focus on is her.

I can't take my eyes off her.

Her face is pale as a ghost. Her pink lips are parted. Her hair is in a messy bun on top of her head.

I continue down her body that has somehow thinned in the hours since I've seen her. When I scan further down, I see why. Blood soaks through a bandage wrapped around her thigh.

A low growl escapes my throat at the sight of her in pain.

"What the hell happened?" I say out loud, but I get no answer.

I step forward, the hands gripping my biceps allowing me. I forget about the men in the room with me. I forget about Maxwell or a plan to escape.

Liesel is in danger. She's been shot, and the wound is not properly closed. She's slowly bleeding to death.

My time is running out.

Her father says something, drawing my attention away from her to the rest of the room. Her father sits at a table with a chessboard in the middle. I don't have any doubt that this man is her real father. The man I met before had dark hair and soft eyes; this man has the same shade of blonde hair as Liesel and cold eyes.

There are a dozen men with guns surrounding every wall in the room. Any one of them could be the one who shot Liesel. Whoever it is, I'm going to find him and kill him, but not after spending weeks torturing him for hurting the woman I love.

Liesel moves, and my eyes cut back to her just in time to see her lips pressed against Corbin's.

What.

The.

Hell.

My brain immediately replays the images of her sucking his cock, but seeing them kissing is worse.

It doesn't make sense.

But when you're in love with someone, your feelings never make any sense.

I'm sure she's kissing him because it's the only way to get Declan back. But it doesn't stop my heart from seizing at the sight.

The kiss starts off simple, a tentative brush of their lips in the same way you might kiss a stranger for the first time, but it quickly evolves into so much more. She's the one who initiates, her tongue sweeping over the seam of his lips, begging for entry.

Corbin hesitates for a moment like he doesn't want this kiss any more than she does.

I narrow my eyes as I study him closer, trying to figure him out. His body is stiff and unmoving. His face isn't flushed, he keeps his eyes open, not closed, and I see no signs of an erection.

As Liesel's tongue pushes between his lips, he stills even more. He can't stand to participate in the kiss.

She pulls back, realizing what she's doing and regretting it.

I don't know why they were told to kiss, but I suspect it has something to do with proving that she no longer loves me. Her father hates me. He wants me dead. He doesn't want me as her husband or lover.

He thinks he can make them kiss, and somehow, her heart will simply start fluttering for another man. He thinks love can be controlled and changed simply by putting two people together and forcing them to hump.

He doesn't know what love is. Love is like jumping off a bridge into the ocean with no idea if it will give you the greatest thrill of your life, kill you on impact, or drown you under the surface. It's a beautiful, magical place that can carry you around the world or destroy you. There is no in-between.

I have no control over whom I love, neither does Liesel. If we did, we wouldn't be together. We would have chosen someone else, someone whose life wouldn't be at risk because we loved each other.

Just as Liesel is about to pull away and decide she can't play this game, Corbin comes to his senses. I know he has to in order to satisfy Liesel's father's twisted demands, but it feels like a betrayal.

He grabs her hips and yanks her to him as their lips clash together. Her mouth is open at the abrupt change, and his tongue slips into her mouth.

She moans like she's trying to convince her body to accept his. At least, that's what I tell myself. She can't possibly be enjoying the kiss.

Their eyes close, and they angle their heads, allowing for a deeper kiss. Their tongues dart in and out of each other's mouths. Liesel's hands grip his shirt, holding him firmly to her, while Corbin's hands slide up and down her hips.

Every move, touch, kiss is like a paper cut to my skin. Tiny little stings singe all over my body, but none of them are deep and merciful enough to finish me off. Watching the woman I love with another man, pretending to care for him, is the worst kind of torture.

I want to run in and save her, but I realize the best way to save her is to watch from a distance. I won't let her die or bleed out, but she's strong enough to do whatever it takes to get her son back. I have to let her take the lead. I have to support her. That's what loving her means right now.

Eventually, I close my eyes, blocking out the sight, but the sound…god, the sound is so much worse. The moans, the sighs, the smacking of their lips together produces worse images in my head than the actual sight.

Suddenly, the sounds stop.

I blink my eyes slowly, allowing them to open.

They are taking their seats back at the table, and her father has a calculating expression. I don't know what he saw when he looked at the two of them together. *Did he see the lies, what they pretended to show him? Or did he see the truth as I did?*

There is no way for Liesel to fall for another man as long as I walk this earth. Even if she wanted to, our love holds us captive. We are in a prison together with unbreakable walls.

I don't know what he sees, but whatever it is, he's pleased with it.

"Let's continue," he says.

He moves a piece on the board.

Then she does.

I'm not much of a chess player. I have no idea who has the advantage or how much longer this will take for her to win. But I have complete confidence she will be victorious.

I want to break out of this room and run and find her. I want to drag her out of here to a safer place. For once, I don't listen to what I want. I don't give in to my protective urges to save her.

Instead, I work on the ropes tying my hands behind my back. I loosen them enough so I can easily slip out of them, but not enough to arouse suspicion from the guards.

Then I watch the screen and wait. I wait for her to win, for her to get her son back. I wait for the moment I'll get them all out of here, praying it comes soon because I'm not sure I'm strong enough to wait very long.

LIESEL

THAT KISS FELT LIKE A DREAM. No, a horrible nightmare. It stirred nothing inside me. My body didn't flush. I didn't grow wetter. I didn't come alive in his arms.

In fact, I was bored as hell kissing him. I had to remind myself of the motions, the mechanics of kissing. I had to remember to make the sounds, to tilt my head, to open my lips wider to allow him in.

It made me realize that if I were to somehow survive my fate, but Langston didn't live on, living without him wouldn't be worth it. I would never again feel alive.

Good thing I won't be surviving then. I'll never have to suffer living in a world without color, a world without Langston. I don't know how I'd endure for even a day.

But Langston will have no choice. I should have been focused on helping him to fall for another woman because not loving me won't be enough. I can't just make him hate me; I have to make him love another woman before I go. Unfortunately, there is very little time to make that happen.

We return to the game, and once again, I'm faced with having to take another piece in order to win the game.

My father notices my hesitation. "From this point forward, we finish the chess game first. Then, you complete all the final challenges at once."

His voice is dripping with wickedness. I don't know what he has planned for me next, but I suspect if he showed me the next challenge now, I wouldn't take another piece. I'd find a way to win without capturing any piece beside his king.

I try to take the possibility of an evil grand finale into account as I continue to play, but I still find myself taking two pieces before I can check his king.

"Check," I say.

He studies the board.

Corbin lets out a breath beside me. I think he's been holding his breath since we kissed, but now his shoulders slump in relaxation.

It's Corbin's reaction that tells me what I already suspect —*I've won.*

"No," my father says.

My heart stops. *Maybe Corbin and I are wrong? Maybe I just lost?*

"Not check; checkmate," my father says with a grin.

I didn't expect him to be so happy that I beat him, but it seems to be what I suspected all along. He wants me to win. He wants me to be strong enough to take over in my son's place. I'm finally close enough to prove it, *but at what cost?*

"Where is Declan?" I say, not trusting my father. I still don't even trust that Declan is truly alive until I lay eyes on my son myself.

"You're right. I think you've earned the right to see your son." My father turns his head to one of his men. "Bring Declan here."

My heart stops. I'm going to see my son.

Time slows as we wait for the guard to return. I don't

know what condition Declan will be in. *Will he be well taken care of? Will he be frail and weak? Scared? Thriving? Sick? Will he think of my father as his own?*

Suddenly, the doors open behind me. I only have to turn around to see him, but I'm terrified of what I will find.

Corbin finds my hand under the table and squeezes. Then together, we both turn and look.

The boy standing in the entryway has my hair, my eyes, my coloring. I have no doubt he's my child, and yet, he looks so much older than Rose or Atlas. He's probably an inch or two taller than Rose, and his hair is gelled back much like my father's. He looks like a small man instead of a boy in dress pants, a gray buttoned-down shirt, and a jacket.

There isn't a speck of dirt on him, nor smudge of food. His clothes are perfectly tidy, like he hasn't played a day in his life.

I don't have to ask questions to know that he's had a strict childhood. Although he's been fed and physically taken care of, he hasn't had a good childhood. It's going to take time to deal with whatever trauma he's experienced since he's been here.

I feel tears watering my eyes, but I blink them back. I can't give in to my emotions. I have to stay strong.

"Declan, come here, boy," my father says.

Declan walks over, easily obeying. His tiny feet glide quickly, not running. He stops at my father's side, and he looks to the table. His eyes grow big at the sight of the chessboard.

"You lost?" he asks my father. "You never lose."

My father puts a hand on Declan's shoulder.

My instinct is to rip his hand clean off for daring to touch my son, but I'd never get away with it.

Patience. Just a little bit longer, and my son will be free of this world.

"I did lose to this woman here."

Declan puts his hand out to me. "Well done. My father is the best chess player I've ever seen. I never beat him. I'm Declan."

I take his hand, and he shakes mine with surprising strength for such a small person.

"I'd love to play against you sometime," he says.

I can't hold the tears back. I let one fall—one drop of everything I've lost and everything I'm about to lose.

"I'd like that," I say.

I quickly wipe away the tear as I see my father studying me for weakness. "What do I have to do?" I stare into my father's eyes.

"Kill."

I glare at his vulgar in Declan's presence. He's too young to be listening to talk about killing, but I also can't bear to have him leave the room. I want to keep my eyes on him, but I have to think about what's best for him, not for myself.

"Declan, would you mind taking my friend Corbin on a small tour while your father and I have a chat?" I ask, deciding it might be best to address Declan directly rather than asking for permission from my father.

Declan looks to Corbin and nods.

We wait until they have left the room before we speak again.

"That was very smart of you to ask Declan instead of me."

"Why? I'm sure you could have told him not to go."

"No. I'm raising a leader, not a follower. I don't give orders. I let him make his own decisions. He knows the world he's in. He's seen danger and death. If he's going to be my heir, he has to learn how to make the right choices."

"He won't be your heir for much longer."

My father leans back in his chair, folding his arms across his chest as he smirks. "You still have two challenges to complete. Two challenges I doubt you are strong enough to endure."

I'm sure he's right, but he underestimates what I'm willing to do for my child.

"What are they?"

"The first is to prove that you can kill."

"Who is my target?"

"Anyone, you can kill anyone. But good luck killing my men; they fight back."

I frown as my eyes circle the room. They all have guns. I have no weapon. I'm outnumbered. It's going to be impossible for me to kill one of them.

"They will, however, have no problem helping you round up Corbin for you to kill him."

I won't kill Corbin. With any luck, he's found a way out of here and has taken Declan with him. But if he hasn't, I have to finish the rest of the challenges.

I have to come up with a plan, a way to kill one of his men even though they have weapons and I have none.

Suddenly, his words resonate in my ear—*prove that you can kill.*

He didn't say to actually kill. He might have meant that, but after I've proven that I can kill, I'll argue the point later.

I take inventory of what I have on my body that I could use—a hair tie, a shirt, jeans, and boots. I don't have much that can be used to kill a person. I need a weapon, *but how to get one?*

I stand from the table and circle the room, looking for my target as a plan forms in my head. I limp a little with each step, exaggerating the appearance of my pain.

I make eye contact with every guard as I circle. Most meet my gaze with a stoic expression, unfazed by the heat in my eyes or the way I puff out my chest. After walking by four, the next man's eyes linger on my chest before giving me a wink.

"You," I say. "I'll kill you."

He laughs, and then the whole room breaks out in laughter. They all see me as a weak woman incapable of harming them. Luckily, that's exactly the attitude I need to be able to gain a weapon and the upper hand.

"Fight me fairly, and we'll see who's stronger," I say.

The man taps his fingers on the outside of his gun strapped across his chest. "We don't have to fight to know."

"I know. I'm stronger." I wink at the man to his left, who laughs at me.

The man I've decided to challenge growls at me. He doesn't like me teasing him. His ego is too small for that, which means I chose my target well. He's just lucky that the first man I plan on killing isn't him. I don't like the idea of killing people, even men who work for the devil. Killing the devil himself; now that's a different story.

"You wouldn't last ten seconds fighting against me, especially not now that you're a cripple."

"Prove it, then."

"What do I gain? Everyone here already knows I can beat you. You're nothing but a weak bitch with an injured leg."

"You get the honor of killing me, of getting rid of me." I look back at my father. "I'm sure my father would look highly on the man who finally got rid of the thorn in his side."

My father nods sternly.

"Fine." The man unhooks his gun and hands it to the guard next to him. As he moves, I get a glimpse of my target. I don't want the big gun. I want the one at his hip, the handgun I've practiced shooting before. He's too much of a coward to remove all of his weapons. I suspect he also has a couple of knives on his body. He won't play fair, which is exactly what I want.

I take a step back as he takes a step forward. I watch as he walks. He's a hulking man, so his movements are slow but forceful. He doesn't think before he moves; he just barrels his way through, used to his size intimidating his foes. That's exactly how he attacks me—barreling forward, throwing his entire body into me as he tries to knock me to the ground.

I let him, not expending energy unnecessarily.

We fall hard to the ground, and I land on my hip.

The men cheer and laugh at how quickly I was knocked down. They think he's going to squash me like a bug.

The toe of his boot hits me hard in the side, kicking me while I'm down. I'm sure it's painful, but I don't feel it with adrenaline flowing through me.

Still, I moan like he's just defeated me with one blow.

More laughter fills my ears.

"Get up, bitch."

I try to get up and then collapse, putting on a good show of weakness.

The man grows impatient. He grabs me by the collar of my shirt and lifts me up until I'm face to face with him. He swings his arm back, ready to hit me hard in the face, but he isn't prepared for me to fight back.

I duck just as he swings. He misses, causing him to stumble forward. We both fall, him on top of me. His body crushes me, but it gives me the access I want. I grab his gun and fire into his shoulder.

I roll out from under the now moaning guard and jump to my feet. I fire in the direction of the man I really want to kill—my father.

The second my bullet whizzes by my father's head, the entire room stops laughing. They grab their guns and aim them at me.

I continue to point my gun at my father.

"Shoot me, and you die," my father says.

"I'm dying either way. At least this way, you die too."

"You have terrible aim. You missed when you had the opportunity to kill me."

"No, I missed on purpose. I want Declan to be completely free of you before I kill you. I don't want your men coming after him his entire life. But if I have to, I'll kill you. Or you can admit that I could if I wanted to and move on to the final challenge."

My father grinds his teeth together. He's furious that he's been outsmarted, but then his face softens. "I accept your terms. You have proven that you can kill. Now it's time for you to actually do it. Bring him in."

I don't have to turn to know who the 'him' is—the only man I've ever loved. The only man who has ever existed for me. The only man I refuse to kill.

LANGSTON

THE MEN in the room grab me as soon as Liesel's father gives the command. I don't put up a fight as they hurry me out with my arms still tied behind my back. I look behind me and don't see Maxwell being dragged in. They left him in the dark room with fewer guards. He'll escape. I've worked my bindings enough that I can get out of it too.

They pull me into the room with Liesel.

Our eyes meet.

We've been in similar situations countless times. Somehow we've survived each time, but this time I don't feel like we are going to be so lucky.

Liesel's standing in the center of the room, holding a gun in her hand. I can see the bandage around her thigh more clearly now. The blood is barely trickling out, which either means the bandage is doing its job, or she's already lost so much blood that there isn't much left to bleed.

I won't let her die.

She has to live.

Whatever it takes.

I tell her that with my eyes. She looks away, not accepting

my promises.

I hope Corbin has found a way to get Declan out of here. Maxwell will break free soon and meet them. They'll run far away from here and hide until Liesel gets free.

I never thought I'd want one of the kids to be taken by Corbin and Maxwell, but she can easily defeat Corbin and Maxwell later; we've done it before. Defeating Liesel's father is going to take more sacrifice than we are willing to make.

Liesel's father stands and walks over to her. He puts his hand on her shoulder, a thinly veiled attempt to control her.

"Your final task is simple. You want Declan to go free and inherit my empire? Then you have to prove that you put my organization and my men first. You have to prove you are strong enough to do the job. You won't allow yourself to love. You won't be selfish or weak. You'll be strong."

Liesel looks at her father, refusing to look at me.

"Prove that you no longer love him and your son goes free. Kill him, and I'll make you the leader of my men."

I don't believe he's just going to let her have control, but I do believe he'll let Declan go. It's clear he doesn't think he's up for the job or he's much too young to take over for an older man. He wants Liesel, and this is how he thinks he's going to get her.

"I need more assurances that Declan will go free. That he's safe," Liesel says sternly.

"Bring in Declan and Corbin," he says.

A few minutes later, they enter. They look well and unhurt. Declan looks sharp in his tailor-made suit. He has stern eyes and stands proudly with his shoulders back. Corbin looks on cautiously. His fists clench, and his pupils dilate. It seems he wants to say something but can't.

Liesel's father walks over and hands Corbin a set of keys and a security card. "The keys are to the black SUV parked behind the building. The security card will gain you access through the building to the back door. It will take you ten minutes to reach the car. The card will only work if Liesel has completed her part of the bargain. If not, you'll be trapped inside."

Corbin looks to Liesel, trying to tell her something. I hope she can read him better than I can because I don't have a clue what he's saying.

"Take the boy and go," Liesel's father says.

Corbin takes the boy's hand, and they leave.

"The clock is now ticking, Liesel." He pulls up his phone with the access code. "If they reach the door and you haven't killed Langston yet, the door will explode when Corbin goes to use the security card."

"No," Liesel gasps.

"Then kill Langston. Kill him, and they go free. Don't, and they die."

Liesel continues to stare at her father instead of me. It takes me a moment to realize why. She finally turns her head my way, and I see the fear in her eyes. Not fear of killing me, though, because I can see in her eyes that she's working on a different plan. Rather, fear that I'm going to try and convince her that she should shoot me.

And she's right.

I will do anything for her—even die for her.

I'll give her a minute to think, but that's it. I've already thought through our options. I can't take on all the men in this room and get to Corbin in time to tell him not to use the security card. We can hope he's smart enough to check for explosive devices before he opens the door. We can hope Corbin will find another way out, but I suspect Liesel's father has already planned for all outcomes. He knows Corbin is in this world. He knows he'll see a trap a mile away.

That only means he's set the trap perfectly. Liesel's father has ensured that Corbin won't get away with Declan unless he allows him to.

There is only one way Declan is getting out of here alive —Liesel has to kill me.

I just don't know how she's getting out of here alive.

She bites her lip, trying to hold back tears. She has a plan to save Declan. She has a plan to save herself.

I smile. Of course, she has a plan. It was my mistake to ever doubt her.

My entire body relaxes and accepts that she's going to live. She's going to live a long and happy life with her kids, with our friends. Someday she'll find someone else to love. Nothing else matters. My death is meaningless because she's going to live.

Shoot me. It's okay. Save him.

She can't help the tear rolling down her cheek, but I just smile at how strong she is. She may not think she's strong enough to survive this, but she is. I wish I could save her from having to be the one who kills me. I'm her killer; she's my huntress. She hunts; I kill.

But I can't kill for her this time. She's always been strong enough; I just wanted to protect her from the pain.

I love you, I mouth.

Then I close my eyes, trying to make it easier on her. I won't feel the pain. I'll just slip off to death.

"Five minutes until they reach the door, possibly less. What will it be?" I hear her father's words.

She's strong. She'll do what she has to.

A bullet hits me. I don't know where on my body because I don't feel a sharp pain. I do feel the wind knocked out of me as I fall backward, though. I don't open my eyes. I don't want Liesel to see me in pain. I don't want her to watch the life leave my body. I want her last memory of me is how much I love her before I drift away.

LIESEL

I WATCH as Langston falls back against the two guards behind him. I don't know if everyone realizes what I did, but I don't have time to wait and see. I have a plan to enact, and time is running out.

I turn the gun on my father. "Deactivate the bomb so Corbin and Declan can get out."

"Not until I'm satisfied that Langston is indeed dead. You'd be surprised by what people can live through." My father is determined to check Langston himself.

As my father walks by me, I pick the cigar lighter from his pocket. Quickly, I grab the bottle of whiskey on the table, pour out its contents, and ignite the liquid—the table bursts into a wall of flames.

The men on the other side of the fire are trapped. They yell and scream as they scramble to attempt to put out the flames and get out of the room.

My father turns and smirks at me. "I didn't think you had it in you. It'll cost you your son's life."

I point the gun at my father. "Deactivate the bomb, or I'll kill you."

He tosses his phone at me; his security app still open on the screen.

My eyes shift to the phone in the air, and I catch it. When I look up again, my father is gone.

One of the men next to Langston is starting to stir. I fire at him before running to Langston.

"Langston! Get up!" I yell.

He opens his eyes, confused as to why he's still alive.

"I didn't shoot you. I shot the guard holding onto you knowing he'd fall backward and bring you with him."

"You're incredible," Langston says wide-eyed before grabbing my neck and pulling me into a kiss. I want this kiss to last forever, but there's not enough time to enjoy even a second of his sweet lips.

"We have to stop Declan and Corbin from using the security card until we've deactivated it," I say. I hold up the phone, and Langston quickly looks it over.

"The app is asking for a passcode. It could take hours to figure out how to hack this," he says.

"We have three minutes, maybe less."

"Shit." Langston jumps up, his mind spinning what to do next.

The fire spits and bursts behind us as it spreads toward us.

"Go," I say, knowing my injured leg will only hold him back from reaching them in time.

"I won't leave without you. I'll stop them, and then I'll come back for you."

I grab his shirt and kiss him quickly one more time. "Go."

Langston jumps up and takes off to find Declan and Corbin.

I start fidgeting with the phone, trying to figure out how to deactivate the bomb, but I don't have a clue.

I cough as the smoke from the fire hits me hard. I need to

get out of here. I run out through the door and run smack into a chest.

"I've got you," Maxwell says. He looks at the fire behind me and coughs. "We need to get out of here."

I shake my head. "We have to deactivate a bomb that's going to go off when Corbin and Declan try to exit the building."

I hand him the phone. "Shit. I'll see what I can do while you find a way out of here."

"Deal."

I lead us down the hallway, following the direction that Langston went after Corbin and Declan. I need to know that Langston got to them in time. I need to know that they are safe.

LANGSTON

I RUN AS FAST as my feet will carry me. I won't fail Liesel. I won't fail Declan. I have to run faster than I've ever run before. The hallways are long and winding, but thankfully there aren't a lot of choices of direction to be made. The only way I'll fail is if I don't run fast enough.

I run faster.

I can't feel my feet as I run. Sweat covers my brow and starts soaking through my shirt. My lungs burn from the exertion, but I only run faster.

I expect to run into some guards, but they all must be back in the room where I left Liesel. Hopefully, the guards are all burning in the fire.

I can't believe Liesel found a way not to kill me. She found a way to save us all. When I started running, I saw Maxwell coming out of the room we were held in and told him to get Liesel out safely. I don't know where her father went, but I'm sure he's running from the fire and carnage. He's a coward. He won't go back to fight his daughter. He's long gone.

Right now, the only fight we have is against the bomb

that might explode, the fire inside, and any of the remaining guards.

We won't fail.

We can't.

We've come this far. We are all going to get out of here alive, and then we are going to live happily ever after together on my island away from all of this.

I don't know if I believe in the powers of manifestation, but I'm willing to try anything.

Run—faster.

Somehow, my body picks up speed, and I see the exit door at the far side still intact, but I don't see Corbin or Declan.

Shit, where are they?

Suddenly, a hand sticks out into the hallway from what seems like a wall, and I come to an abrupt stop. A panel in the wall fully opens, and Corbin appears, a boy I assume is Declan behind him.

"The door is...boobytrapped," I say, breathing hard, barely able to get the words out.

"We know; that's why we are hiding here," Corbin says.

I let out a big breath. "We have to get Declan out of here. The building is on fire, and Liesel's father took off."

Corbin nods. "Know of any other exits? Or do we need to deactivate the bomb?"

"Run!" I hear Liesel yelling from behind me.

"Shit," I say when I see guards running behind her and Maxwell, followed by flames.

It seems our decision is made for us. We don't have time to deactivate the bomb. I look at Declan.

"Do you know a safe way out of here?" I ask him.

"Why should I tell you?" Declan puffs his chest out.

"You're going to die if you don't."

"I'm not afraid of death."

"I believe that, but I have a secret. I know who your brother and sister are, and they'd very much like to meet you."

"I don't have any siblings."

"Their names are Rose and Atlas. You can meet them if you show us how to get out of here."

Declan considers. "This way." He slips past Corbin and me and starts running away from the flames.

Liesel and Maxwell are catching up, but they are still a good thirty seconds behind us. "Run!" Liesel shouts.

I want to stay with Liesel, but we need to get Declan out. That has to be the priority, and he's already taken off through another hidden panel in the wall that leads to a tunnel.

"Here," Corbin says, tossing me a gun.

I catch it as we continue to chase after Declan. The tunnel is dark, but it doesn't stop Declan from running full speed ahead. The boy isn't afraid of anything; I'll give him that.

I hear footsteps behind us, and I know Liesel and Maxwell have made it to the entrance of the tunnel; thank god.

Then Declan is at a door at the end of the tunnel.

"Wait!" I yell.

Declan stops.

"Step back, Declan. Let me see if it's got explosives rigged to it," Corbin says as he's closer to the door.

Declan doesn't move, so I yank him back as Corbin inspects the door carefully. "It's clear. Let's go."

Corbin pushes open the door, and streetlights shine on us. I grab Declan just as bullets start raining down on us from outside.

I turn him around, so my body shields him from the gunfire. Corbin and I start returning fire out the door.

The gunshots are limited, which means only one, maybe two, people are shooting at us.

"There's an SUV parked to the left," Corbin says as he tosses me some car keys.

I have to get Declan out of here, then come back for the rest of them.

"Go, I'll cover you," Corbin says as I inch toward the exit.

We both pop out onto the street at the same time. Corbin fires, and I run with Declan in my arms to the car.

The block is nearly a block away, but Corbin's fire is enough to get us there safely. I unlock the car with the key fob, hop in, and gently toss Declan into the backseat as I turn the car on.

"Stay down," I tell him as I drive the block back to collect everyone else. Suddenly, there's an explosion, and the entire building erupts up in flames.

"NO!" I yell as I watch the building burn.

Declan sits up in the backseat and looks out at the building in flames. I suspect this building has been his home his entire life. It's gone in a second; everyone he knows —gone.

Carefully, I drive toward the exit from which we just escaped. There is a body burning; I suspect Corbin's.

I grab my gun. I can't go without knowing for sure if Liesel is…

I can't even think it.

"Declan," I say.

The boy looks at me with big eyes. He's in shock.

"Look at me. I need you to keep your head down. I'll be right back, you hear me? I'll be right back. Stay hidden."

I wait until he crouches down on the car floor, then I run into the flames.

The smoke hits me first, and I cough over and over.

There is no oxygen here, but I have enough left in my lungs to yell for Liesel. "Liesel!"

I get no response.

The flames flicker around me. I crawl down low to try to avoid the smoke, but it's everywhere.

I open my mouth, but it lets in too much smoke. I cough relentlessly, trying to get the smothering fumes out of my lungs. My hands reach out and make contact with a body—a body that is more ash than human flesh at this point.

"Liesel?" I beg.

Please, it can't be.

But then I see the strands of blonde hair.

"No," I whisper as my heart shatters. "Please, god, no."

But it's her. I know it's her—*Liesel's dead.*

"I'll protect them. I'll love them as my own as I loved you. As I'll always love you."

It takes all the strength I have to move away from her body, but I do. I have to. I have to get back to Declan before anyone who survived discovers him.

I run back out of the still-burning building and jump into the car.

Declan is still in the backseat where I left him.

I cough, unable to speak. I start driving. I can't think of where I should drive; I just know I have to drive away. Once we're a safe distance away, I'll call for someone to pick us up.

The boy in the backseat shakes as I drive, but I don't know how to comfort him. I don't know how to explain to him that he just lost his mother. And although I want to be his father, I just failed him.

A car pulls out in front of me, and I slam on the breaks. We stop just short of hitting the car, but Declan isn't buckled in and flies forward. I put my arm out to stop him from flying through the windshield.

At that moment, my heart flips. He becomes my son in an

instant. Being a father is the most natural thing in the world to me. I wrap him in my arms and pull him onto my lap.

I may have failed Liesel, but I won't fail him.

"You're safe. I've got you. I've got you, Declan. I won't let anyone hurt you. You're safe."

LANGSTON

SHE'S DEAD.

I still can't accept it.

Liesel is gone, burned in the fire.

The feel of her charred flesh is seared into my memory. The singed ends of her blonde hair turned black will haunt me for the rest of my days. It's not how I want to remember her. In some ways, it's better that I saw her body. I'm not sure I would ever believe she is really dead if I hadn't seen her myself.

Still, my heart still can't process that she's gone. Once again, I failed her.

I haven't stopped crying since we left the shattered building. I continued weeping the entire flight home with Declan in my lap. You'd think my tears would dry now that we've landed on my island, but they still fall just as freely. I can't imagine a time when I won't be crying. From now on, I'll see the world in shades of black, white, and gray. My world will be void of color.

The only love I'll ever feel again is for my children. I'll

never remarry. I'll never fall in love. I'll never have my soul be connected to another woman ever again.

My heart wishes I were dead. The loss is suffocating. It's the worst pain I've ever felt. I don't know how I'm going to endure a lifetime of it.

Then I look down at my lap, where Declan has fallen asleep with his head on my thigh. I stroke his hair. This is how I'll survive the pain—by taking care of the children she gave her life to protect.

I'll remember Liesel in Rose's hair and bravery, in Atlas's eyes and intelligence, and in Declan's strength. She'll never really be gone as long as they live.

The plane comes to a stop. Carefully, I lift Declan up in my arms. He doesn't stir. He's too exhausted from the day he's had. I wish I could sleep as easily as him. He can sleep away his pain, while nothing will be able to push my own heartache away.

I carry him off the plane and see a car waiting with Siren standing outside. I wasn't able to tell them much, just that I had Declan and I would arrive tonight, but it's not surprising they figured out what my lack of mention of Liesel meant. They sent my best friend to help me.

The second I step foot on the ground, Siren runs toward me and pulls me into her arms while I'm still holding Declan.

I sob into her shoulder, unable to bear the anguish of what I've lost. She helps me collapse to the ground, careful not to disturb Declan as she holds me in her arms. I don't know how I'm ever going to find the strength to stand again.

Siren starts humming. I don't recognize the tune, but it sounds sad and lonely. I don't know why she's humming such a sad song. Maybe she thinks it will soothe my soul to hear something that so clearly matches how I'm feeling. Instead, it drives me further into sadness.

More tears fall.

My body shakes.

Her arms wrap around me tighter as her voice gets louder.

I want to tell her to stop singing, that it's not helping me, but I don't want to upset her. I glance down and am surprised that Declan hasn't woken up with how loud she's humming now.

Her voice changes from hums to words. The song speaks of slipping away, of missing her. It takes me a minute to place the song before I realize she's singing 'Slipped Away' by Avril Lavigne. It's a fitting song I feel down to my bones. I don't know how Siren was able to conjure up a song that fits my feelings so clearly, but I can't take much more of the sadness. There is no escaping my agony right now, but I can't handle it flooding all of my senses at once.

Wait.

Siren. Is. Singing.

My eyes widen as I stare at Siren. She's not struggling to sing. Her voice is back better than ever. There is no sign that singing is bringing her pain. She's healed. She's regained what was lost.

I realize then that her singing isn't to put my heart's emotions into words; she's singing to remind me that not all is lost. I should have hope.

Liesel is dead; there is no hope.

But my heart clings to the tiniest bit of hope as I listen to Siren sing. She shouldn't be able to sing like this, not so soon after her injury. The doctors weren't sure if she would ever speak again, let alone sing. And yet, she's singing.

Siren grabs my elbows and helps me stand while I continue to hold Declan in my arms. She walks me to the car, still singing. She helps me into the front passenger seat as I hold Declan in my lap. Then she climbs into the driver's seat.

She never lets there be a moment without her humming or singing on the drive back. I realize now how comforting it is. I can't speak, and nothing she could say would bring me any comfort. She fills the silence with her songs—all sad, melancholy songs about love and loss.

As we get closer to the house, though, she speaks.

"Everyone knows already. They want to be there for you, but if your grief is too much to handle being around anyone, let me know, and they'll give you space until you're ready."

I don't know what I want. I should do whatever is best for Declan, Rose, and Atlas, but I don't even know what that is. Declan has just been ripped from the only world he knew. Rose and Atlas barely even knew Liesel. I don't know if any of them need to deal with the pain of her loss today.

Siren doesn't ask again. She studies me carefully after stopping the car in front of the house.

Everyone is standing on the porch, looking at us with somber expressions as we pull up. My heart bleeds as they walk over, not ready to face what happened but knowing I don't want to push them away either. The only thing worse than facing my grief is facing it alone. Luckily, I won't have to do that.

I'm engulfed with hugs as I step out of the car with Declan in my arms. I'm afraid he's going to wake up with everyone hugging us, and I'm going to have to introduce him to everyone. I'm going to have to talk—that's not something I'm capable of at the moment.

Declan sleeps through it all, and it makes me wonder what he went through before to be this exhausted.

As we all walk into the house, I know I need to make some decisions—where I want to sleep, where Declan should sleep, if I want Rose and Atlas to come to greet me. Yet somehow, I never have to make a decision.

Enzo leads the way, opening doors and speaking solemn commands to Zeke and Beckett. Kai and Siren walk on either side of me. Siren's strokes Declan's hair, soothing him when he starts to stir until he falls back asleep.

I don't know what's happening until I enter the house and see the living room has been turned into one giant mattress. All the mattresses in the house have been brought down, along with pillows and blankets thrown everywhere.

"We're going to all sleep down here together. No one has to be alone tonight," Siren says.

It feels right.

For the first time, I truly look into the eyes of all of my friends. All of them are dripping with tears. They were Liesel's friends. They felt the loss too.

The men start carrying the kids down the stairs. It's past their bedtime, so they're all groggy. If they wake up, they probably won't remember moving downstairs.

Enzo and Zeke lie their kids down on one of the mattresses on the side, and then Kai and Siren carry down Atlas and Rose. Atlas stirs awake in Siren's arms.

"Dad?" he says, but his eyes are still closed.

"I'm here. Sleep, we can talk in the morning." I kiss his forehead.

"Okay," he yawns.

I walk over to Kai, who is holding Rose. I kiss my daughter's forehead as well.

They place both of the kids on one of the center mattresses. I walk over and sit down next to them with Declan still in my arms. I'm not sure I can let him go tonight. I don't want him to wake up afraid.

Then I spot Phoenix on the outskirts of the room. She

searches the room for her brothers, but she's not going to find them. I need to tell her what happened.

I lie Declan down next to Atlas, careful not to wake him, before walking over to Phoenix.

We stare at each other, unsure of how to act. Our relationship is strained; I'm not sure if it will ever be repaired.

But right now, we both lost the most important people to us.

"I'm sorry," I say.

"I'm sorry, too," she croaks back.

Then we collapse in each other's arms, both grieving enormous loss. Everyone else is crying, but not like us. We each lost a piece of our souls, not just a close friend. There is no consoling us; I don't know how we'll ever stop.

Somehow we have to stop. I'm the kids' father, and as far as Rose and Atlas are concerned, she's the only mother they will ever really know. We have to find a way through this pain. We have to find a way back to them.

Someone must have moved us both to a bed because the next thing I know, I'm cocooned with my kids on one side, Phoenix next to them, and Siren on my other. The rest of my friends, my family, sleeping on various mattresses around us.

Despite my grief, the strong pull of slumber eventually pulls me under, granting me a moment of relief, at least until the morning comes and I have to endure all over again.

LANGSTON

"ARE YOU DEAD?" Rose asks, pulling one of my eyelids up.

I wince at light hits my swollen eye.

"No," I reply.

She's sitting on top of me, tilting her head to the side as she studies me. "Sick then? You slept past lunchtime."

I frown.

I should have woken up earlier. I should have been there to explain to my kids what happened the second they woke up. Instead, it's day one without Liesel, and I'm already failing.

I grab my pounding head as I sit up and look around. The room is quiet, despite how many people are in it. Everyone is sitting on the various mattresses holding scattered plates with a few bites of food, hard liquor drinks, and used tissues.

Rose is sitting on my legs, *but where is Atlas? Where is Declan?*

Siren must realize my alarm because she lifts Atlas up over her legs, so he's sitting right next to me. Then, she nods silently for me to look to my other side.

Declan is snoring next to me.

My heart relaxes. All the kids are safe.

"So you're sick?" Rose asks again.

"Yes, I'm heartsick."

She scrunches her nose. "What does that mean?"

"It means my heart is broken. You remember Liesel? Your other mother?"

Both kids nod.

"She…" I can't say the words. Why can't I say the words?

She's dead.

Just say it. Tell them. They deserve to know that their mother is dead.

But I can't say it. Not yet. I can't. I just can't.

"She wasn't able to come back with us, and it makes me sad."

Rose takes my hand. "I miss her."

"I miss her, too."

Siren gives me a smile. None of the adults in the room argue with me about my decision. It's too hard for them to talk about too.

Then Rose looks down at Declan. "Is he dead?"

"No, he's sleeping. He had a long night."

"Who is he? He kind of looks like Atlas but with neater hair and slightly bigger," Rose says.

This draws Atlas' attention, and he peers over at the sleeping boy as well.

I open my mouth, so not ready to have this conversation. *How do I explain everything to them? How do I explain everything to Declan when he wakes up? What is he going to be like when he wakes up?* He trusted me last night because he had no choice. I'm not sure if he'll feel the same way today. I'm a complete stranger to him.

Luckily, I don't have to worry about that. It seems that the kids will solve those problems on their own.

"I'm Declan."

"I'm Rose, and this is my brother Atlas."

They all stare at each other a moment, and then Atlas says, "You're our brother. We're triplets. We are going to be best friends, and you'll learn to love Rose."

"Hey, don't act like I'm hard to love," Rose says.

Atlas laughs.

Declan looks back and forth between them. His eyes are big, entranced by them.

"Come see my room, Declan. You can sleep there until dad gets you your own room," Atlas says, grabbing Declan's hand. Then they all run upstairs.

Just like that, they become siblings.

I'm not sure Declan fully understands what's going on, but he didn't protest when they dragged him upstairs. We'll talk more later.

"Here." Siren hands me a shot glass after the kids run upstairs.

"Should I be drinking at a time like this?"

"What else should you be doing? It will numb the pain."

I throw the shot back, not even registering what kind of liquor is in it. Siren pours me another shot, and I take that one too.

"Do you want any food?"

I shake my head. Alcohol is the only thing I can stomach. I don't think I can chew food. I grab the bottle from Siren and start working on it.

"I know now isn't the time for talking, but if you need us to do anything, we're ready," Enzo says. I notice he has his own bottle of whiskey, and his eyes are already bloodshot.

I nod as I lift the bottle to my lips before I realize the answer. I put the bottle down abruptly.

"We have to go back."

"I thought the explosion killed everyone?" Enzo asks.

"It did, but I need to make sure…" I can't say Liesel's

119

name. "I need to make sure her father is dead and that he has no successors to take over whatever is left of his organization."

"When do you want to leave?"

All eyes in the room are on me. Everyone in this room will do whatever I want. They won't judge me. There is no judgment in watching someone grieve. We all grieve differently. Whatever I need, they'll do.

I hear laughter from the kids upstairs. For the first time since my world ended, I smile. They will never have to experience my grief. I can protect them from the worst. What's most important now is to ensure they are completely safe. Ensure the man who took their mother is dead. Ensure they are safe forever.

I take another sip, knowing I'm going to have to stop drinking soon. I need to be sober enough to do what I need to do.

"Tonight."

LANGSTON

Siren and Enzo agree to go with me back to Moscow, the rest deciding they should stay to protect the kids. Siren insisted she come, and Enzo didn't even give me the option. But of course, they would be the ones I would choose to come with me. They had the closest relationship to Liesel. They are the closest to me.

My head pounds on the flight back.

"Here," Siren says, handing me a bottle of scotch.

"I shouldn't drink. I'm going to need to be sober if I have to fight."

"You won't survive the flight if you don't drink." She nudges the bottle at me. "Enzo and I are sober enough. If he's alive, we'll kill him. There is no one here you need to protect. Drink; stop feeling."

I take the bottle and do as she says. She's right—it numbs the pain. My hands stop trembling. My heart settles. It's almost like I need the drug in order to be sober.

I can't live like this forever, but for today the alcohol is necessary.

"Do you want to talk?" Enzo asks, staring at me.

121

Everyone here has thought they lost the person they loved most at one point or another. I'm the only one who actually has lost that person.

I don't want to talk.

And yet, I do.

The words spill out of me.

"The first time I met her, she was hunting for a spider. I called her huntress. She hunted but couldn't kill, so I had to kill the spider for her." I smile, thinking of the memory. It seems that when you reach the end, your mind decides to go back to the beginning.

"I became her killer. We lost so much time we could have spent together. Somehow, even in that lost time, I have the best memories of her. We hated each other. We loved each other. We tried to kill each other, and we protected each other."

Tears well again, but I continue.

"I'll never find another woman so infuriating and so wonderful. I'll never love again like I loved her. And I'll take the pain. I'll take it all after tonight because I want to remember her. I don't want to be afraid to talk about her. I want to remember everything. I want my kids to know their mother. We have to tell her story. We can't be afraid of the pain."

Enzo smiles at me, reflecting on his memories of Liesel.

"She was the biggest bitch. She wanted me for my money and to fuck with you. I hated her. And yet, when she thought no one was watching, she would do something so kind, so incredible that I thought she had a twin sister who was an angel.

"I remember one time, my father caught me with stolen drugs. She took his wrath. She paid the price so I wouldn't have to," Enzo says through his tears. He holds up a bottle. "To Liesel."

We all clink our bottles and then take a sip.

"She hated me because she thought you loved me more than her. At least, at first, she did. She knew we were soulmates and best friends, and yet, she was so convinced she was the right woman for you, not me. She knew. She always knew, even when she pretended to hate me. We may be best friends, but you and she were two halves of the same heart," Siren says.

"I could only be friends with you because of her love for you. She loved you enough to not be jealous of our friendship. She knew that she had captured your entire being when you were five years old, so it didn't matter that we were friends. Us being friends wasn't a threat; I couldn't steal your heart even if I had wanted to. It already belonged to Liesel."

She clinks her bottle with ours again. "To Liesel," she says with a smile.

"To the only woman I hated and loved in equal measure. I love you, Liesel—my huntress, my wife, mother of my children, my everything. I'll carry you with me always so I can't miss you. I'll never let you leave me."

I clink my bottle one more time to theirs, and we all drink.

Then we change our focus to what we're going to do when we get back to Moscow. We discuss the layout, the likely scenarios. We prepare for war, knowing we are probably only going to find the remnants of an explosive fire that burned the building and everyone inside to death.

We reach the compound as dusk settles over the city. There is still smoke billowing from the building even though it's been over a day since I left.

There are no signs of life.

No people digging through the rubble. No squatters. Nothing but death.

I lead Enzo and Siren back to the spot where I last saw Liesel's body, but we find nothing.

"Are you sure this is where you last saw her?" Siren asks.

I nod and kneel down to get a better look. I find a few strands of her blonde hair, just like before. But this time, there is no body attached.

Enzo and Siren pick up pieces of fabric, threads of shirts similar colored to the ones Corbin and Maxwell were wearing, and hand them to me.

All signs that they are indeed dead.

"The fire must have raged so intensely that it burned their bones," Enzo says.

I nod. It's still hot.

"We need to find Liesel's father. We need to make sure he's dead."

We walk through the debris, spreading out to look for any clues as to who lived and who died.

We don't find any bodies, though. They all burnt up.

I walk to the far edge of the wreckage when I finally spot a body.

The body is badly burned. I can't make out any facial features, but once again, there's a clothing thread. I pick it up, adding to the collection of other items we can test for DNA and bury to give our lost ones some type of burial. It's the thick dark fabric of Liesel's father's coat.

"Did you find him?" Siren asks.

I nod.

"We should go back home," I say.

I hold all the items in my hand—the three pieces of fabric and a lock of Liesel's hair.

I scan the debris one more time, but these are the only personal items we find. A strange feeling overcomes me.

Strange that in a field of debris, we only found items

belonging to the four people whose living status we need to know.

Strange that we found no bodies.

Strange that we found no evidence of anyone else.

Strange that it feels like this evidence was planted.

Strange.

And hopeful.

I don't think Liesel's father is dead. I don't think Corbin or Maxwell is dead. I don't think Liesel is dead.

I stare at my friends. They won't believe me. They'll think I'm delusional and I'm inventing theories because I can't handle my grief. I need more proof.

I grin. I'll do whatever it takes to find the truth. I'll search to the ends of the earth. My huntress is alive. She lived. Now it's my turn to hunt for her, to survive long enough to save her like she's saved me.

21

LIESEL

I HAVE no question who set off the explosion—my father. He'd rather see us dead than let us escape.

I cough up blood and soot after the explosion knocks me to the ground.

Declan.

Langston.

I don't process the damage done to my own body. All I care about is whether or not my boys made it out. I force my head up to try to look to the door, but I can't see anything through the billowing smoke.

They had to have made it.

I remember the last thing I saw was them exiting through the door. It was several seconds before the explosion happened. They are safe.

My head collapses, and my face hits the ground with a thud. I don't feel the sharp pain of the rocks sticking into my face. I don't feel anything.

I'm dying.

Even before this happened, the wound in my leg was a death sentence unless I got medical attention fast. Whatever damage added to my body will just quicken my death. All I can wish for now is confirmation that Declan and Langston made it out alive before I slip away.

As if the universe decides to answer my wish, Langston appears before me. I must be hallucinating, but then I feel his touch against my hair.

I don't move.

I don't breathe.

I beg my heart to stop beating.

He can't know I'm alive. I have to stay here to ensure my father is dead with whatever little time I have left, and he needs to get Declan out of here.

Langston stays for a moment. I can hear his sobs and feel his pain emanate off his body as he continues to touch my hair. He must think I'm dead. I don't want to imagine what the rest of my body looks like for him to assume that so easily without checking for breathing or my pulse.

I could put Langston out of his misery. I could speak, move, let him know that I'm alive. But it would only ensure he suffers more pain when he eventually lost me anyway, when he couldn't save me.

It's better for him to let me go now.

He touches my hair one more time, and then he's gone.

Feeling Langston gone is what gets me. The tears start, but not because I lost him. I got to love Langston before my life ended, and that was worth everything it cost me. He's the father of my children. I don't care that he isn't theirs by blood; he's theirs by love.

Once I'm convinced he's gone, I try to stand up. I need to kill my father. I need to destroy the last threat against my children. My body refuses, but I've never listened to what my body wants. My heart is the only thing that matters, and my heart isn't injured. My heart is strong, strong enough to stay alive long enough to destroy my father.

I don't know how I get to my feet, just that I do.

I see bodies lining the hallway, but I don't linger to look at them. I quickly see the blood, the ash, the carnage. I don't know if any of them are alive or dead, friend or enemy. I just know that I have to find my father and kill him.

After walking down a few hallways, I begin to lose consciousness again. I succeed in finding my father, just not in killing him.

———

I wake in a dark cell complete with bars, a damp floor, and a thin mattress on the floor. I don't remember how I got here. I remember finding my father and then nothing.

I failed.

I don't know how much time I have left to succeed.

"You're finally awake," a deep voice says.

I look in the direction of the voice, but the room is too dark to make out who is in the cell next to me.

"Who are you?"

"You don't recognize my voice?" he chuckles.

It takes me a second but then I place it. "Corbin?"

I race over to the side of the cell he's on. I reach my hand through the bars, and he takes my hand in his. I can't believe I'm thankful that Corbin is in the next cell over.

I have so many questions to ask, and I don't know which is most important to ask first.

"How long have I been out?"

Corbin opens his mouth to answer, but I'm already asking the next question.

"Where are we?

"Where is my father?

"Have you found a way out yet?

"What about killing my father?

"Are you hurt?

"What about Maxwell?

"How am I still alive?

"What about Langston? The kids?"

Corbin reaches through the bars and squishes my lips together to shut me up.

"If you'll stop talking, I'll tell you everything I know."

I nod.

He lets go of my lips.

"You tried to attack your father after the explosion. I don't know what you thought you were going to be able to do in the physical state you were in, but I saw you hunt for him, and I followed you. You got a good punch in before he knocked you out with some drug."

That's why my head is spinning.

"His men did the same to me, and I suspect Maxwell. He's in the cell on the other side of you, but he's in really bad shape. He hasn't woken up yet."

"What about you?" I ask.

"My left leg is badly burnt, third-degree if I had to guess. I suffered a concussion and a few broken ribs, but nothing I won't recover from. I've been in here for over two weeks. You just arrived here yesterday."

"Where have I been all this time?"

"The hospital. You had surgery. You got skin grafts for the burns, a cast for your broken wrist, and pain medication. A nurse came in this morning and injected you with some drugs. Your father wants you to live, unlike Maxwell and me. He gave us the minimal amount of medical attention to keep us alive."

I study my body. I have on loose-fitting pajama pants, a cotton shirt, and slippers on my feet. My body looks clean, and I feel several bandages on my legs and arms. There's a cast on my left wrist. I feel a dull ache, but nothing too intense, which means pain medicine is still pumping through me.

"Is Maxwell going to make it?" I ask.

"I don't know. From what I can tell, he's been torched all over his body too. He has an IV providing him nourishment, but that's all I can tell until he wakes up."

"Let me see what I can see." I start to move away, but Corbin grabs my arm.

"Langston and the kids are safe."

"How do you know?" I can hear my heart pounding in my chest. I saw Langston escape with my own eyes before everything went dark, but I need all the evidence I can get.

"Your father talks about them. He doesn't want them; he wants you. But it won't stop him from trying to use them as leverage to get what he wants from you."

"Where are we?"

"Not sure. We were all unconscious and woke up down here. We could still be in Russia or a thousand miles away."

"We have to kill him."

He nods. "I agree. We need to come up with a plan."

"I'm going to check on Maxwell. We need to know how many people we have on our side."

I slide across my small cell. It can't be more than ten feet by ten feet. "Maxwell?" I ask through the bars.

No answer.

I'm able to see what Corbin described—burns cover his skin, and there's an IV in his arm. I watch his chest rise and fall and compare it to my own.

"His breathing is slightly slower than mine, but he's alive and unconscious. I don't know what we could do to help."

"Nothing. Either he'll wake up on his own, or he won't."

I sigh as I sit back on my bed and lean against the wall. I'm about to ask Corbin if he has any ideas for an escape or how to kill my father when he speaks.

"I'm sorry."

"Why? This isn't your fault," I reply.

Corbin leans against the same wall next to me, with the bars separating us. He lets out a large sigh, seeming to relax.

"No, but I assumed the reason you were going after your father was because you wanted his power for yourself. I knew the men you're friends with. The Black family seeks power and money at all costs. At least, that's how it used to be before Kai took over. I thought you were working with your father to gain their trust and overthrow my family before taking over for your father. I thought you were playing us all."

"And now?" I ask cautiously.

"I know you love Langston. You love your kids. You hate your father for what he's done to your family. I know you just want him dead. You want to watch his business burn. You're not your father's daughter."

He takes a deep breath. "I'm sorry for my part in hurting you. After this is all over...when we kill your father and escape, I won't punish you. I won't take you hostage. And I won't come after your kids. I—"

"No," I stop him.

He frowns. "No? I'm telling you that our deal is off. I'll help you kill your father, but I don't want you as my hostage. You're free of our deal. If we survive this, then you get to live your life with the man you love and your kids."

"No, I don't think I'm going to survive this. Even with the best medical care, we both know my destiny. I can't let Langston love me again. He thinks I'm dead. We can't let anything change that. I can't let him go through my death twice."

"So, what do you want from me?"

"If we somehow manage to survive this, then I want you to take me as your hostage."

"You can live with me, of course, but I'm not so cruel as to take you hostage."

"You have to. If I live long enough, I'll want to run straight into Langston's arms once I'm free. You have to stop me from doing that; make it so I can't get to him. Promise me."

Corbin runs his hand through his hair before his head falls back. I know he's trying to think of another solution, a way he doesn't have to keep his promise, but he can't think of one. And he owes me.

"I promise," he finally says.

I relax, knowing that I won't have to put Langston through my death again. I have a plan. I'll only have to break his heart once.

And for now, that's enough.

———

The door to my cell pops open, and the creek it makes pulls me out of a dreamless sleep.

I sit up and come face to face with my father.

"Brave of you to come into my cell on your own," I say, noticing he's brought no men into the cell with me.

"It is brave of me. I know you'll try and kill me any chance you get. Lucky for me, the nurse just gave you another shot of pain medication while you were sleeping to further sedate you. You don't have the strength to fight me."

He's right. Simply sitting up like this is taking all of my energy. I'm not even sure I have the strength to stand.

"What do you want?"

"I just want to have an honest chat, you and I." He sits down on a folding chair he's brought into my cell.

I glance over at Corbin, who is either asleep or pretending to be.

"I'll make this simple for you, my daughter. Do as I say, and I won't go after Declan or either of your other kids."

"I already won the game. I did as you say. The deal was Declan went free, and I got your empire, not locked up in a cell."

"Don't pretend like you completed the final challenge. We both know Langston is still alive."

I swallow. Would my children be safer if Langston were dead? No, I refuse to accept that. I won't kill Langston, no matter what my father says he needs from me to not go after my children.

"What do you want?"

"The same thing I've always wanted—to know you are strong enough to be the leader my men need. I need to know you'll put them and the power that comes with it before anything else. You can't still be in love with that man and do this job."

"Why is it so important you have a successor?"

He stares but doesn't answer.

"You're dying, aren't you? You don't have much time left. You don't have time to wait for Declan to grow up. You need someone to take over now."

"It doesn't matter why. You will do what I say, prove that you can do the job, then I'll let your kids live."

"So you want me to kill Langston?"

He nods. "Prove that you no longer love him."

"No," I say, knowing that Langston has all three kids on his island with our friends and their resources. My kids are safe. I don't care what torture my father inflicts on me. I'll survive long enough to kill him or watch him die from whatever illness he has.

"I'll let you have some time to think about it." He stands up and stops at the door. "Stop loving him, or I'll go after your children. I'll kill the other two, who aren't up for the job, and hand everything I own to Declan when he turns eighteen. I'm a patient man. I can wait for your answer. You have a year until I go after your first child. Two years until I go after your second. And over a decade before I go after your third. Is loving him really worth sacrificing your children? I'd stop loving him now if I were you and save us all some time."

He clinks the door of my cell shut.

"If you want me to consider it, then ensure Maxwell and Corbin live. Give them proper medical treatment. If either of them dies, then I won't consider your offer at all. Call it a good-faith gesture."

My father glares at me, grinding his teeth together so hard and loud in his rage. Finally, he gives me a curt nod.

I saved Corbin and Maxwell. My children are safe with Langston. Now, if I could only find a way to kill my father while saving myself.

2 2

LANGSTON

ONE YEAR Later

I hold my cup of coffee in my hand, drinking it quietly on the deck while Atlas, Declan, Ellie, and Cayden eat their breakfast. Rose and Finn aren't early birds and won't be up for another hour. Most of the adults are milling about in various parts of the house. I'm the only one who has been up for hours. I don't sleep, not anymore. Not while I'm separated from Liesel.

I've taken the duty of feeding the kids breakfast in the morning. The house I originally built as Liesel and I's dream house has become our safe haven. Everyone moved here. Siren and Zeke are building a house nearby. Kai and Enzo sleep on one of the yachts parked just off the shore. Phoenix sleeps in the part of the house I designed for her. Beckett sleeps in one of the guest bedrooms, and all the kids sleep here in the main house with me more often than not.

It works.

We're safe here on our own private island. We control who comes and who leaves. The seclusion does make it harder to search for a man who doesn't want to be found, though.

He's haunted my dreams to the point that I think I must be deluding myself into thinking he's still alive. He must have burned in the fire just like everyone else. That's why we haven't found him.

But if that's true, if he's really dead, then that means Liesel is too. If she were alive and her father was dead, she would have come back. She would have been free.

He has to be alive. I can't handle him not being alive. I can't face the reality that Liesel is probably dead, and that's why I haven't found her either.

Either way, I won't stop searching until I have definite proof. I can't stop searching, not if there is a chance she's alive.

"Go for a run with me?" Zeke asks as he steps foot on the deck.

I nod, knowing it's better to answer without words. Zeke's hearing still hasn't fully recovered, although he is healing. Or he's getting better at reading lips.

Kai takes over watching the kids while Zeke and I quickly stretch and then start running down the beach. Every morning I run with Zeke. Every evening I run with Enzo. Every afternoon I swim with Kai. And every evening after I put the kids to bed, I drink with Siren. It's become a bit of a routine. Beckett is the only one who doesn't have a specific task in taking care of me and ensuring I don't have a moment to think about Liesel. His focus is more on security, but he tends to fill in whenever someone needs a break.

Running with Zeke on the beach is just a normal morning here. Occasionally, I take a small team to go follow a lead when we think we've found Liesel's father, but otherwise, we are here, living a dream life on our own private island.

"Did you follow that lead in India?" I ask as we jog, our bare feet hitting the sand with each step.

"Yes, it was a dead end."

I sigh. "Beckett thought he had something in Chile that he wanted to follow up on. Hopefully, that will lead to more clues."

"Can I be honest with you?"

This can't be good. "Sure. You've upended your whole life for me. I think you have the right to be honest with me."

He stops running.

I take a couple more steps before I stop too. *This really can't be good.*

He puts his hands on his head like he's struggling to breathe, but really he's struggling to get his words out. "It's been over a year. We have everyone searching for any sign of them. His organization has gone silent. His money is tied up in banks, motionless. Every clue leads to him being dead."

I know he's right, but I can't accept it.

He puts his hand on my shoulder. "I'm sorry. If I were in your shoes, I wouldn't stop looking either. I'd never stop looking for Siren. I shouldn't have said anything."

"No, you should have. Don't be afraid to speak what's on your mind. I need to hear what you all are thinking. It's not just me I have to worry about. I have to think about the kids too."

"Race you back?"

I grin, taking off, knowing I'm much faster than him. He's almost twice my size. He can beat me at lifting weights, but not this.

It feels good to run this fast. It makes me feel alive when I mostly feel lost, dead, empty. I don't know what I'd do if it weren't for everyone ensuring I eat, drink, and shower every day. If they didn't plan every second of my day, I'm pretty sure I'd be homeless and wasted away to nothing. It's these little moments that keep me living.

I beat Zeke back to the house easily when I spot Siren walking down the steps leading to the beach.

"Looking for your husband? He'll be back in another five minutes. You know his slow ass can't keep up with me."

She smiles. "Actually, I was looking for you."

"Wanting to get a drink early? Or are you swapping your time for Kai's?"

She laughs. "I guess we have established a bit of a babysit-ting routine, but no. Actually, we found a clue. We think we found Liesel's father."

My eyes go wide. Usually, when anyone brings me any evidence, they try to say it in the most subdued, pessimistic way as to not get my hopes up.

"Where is he? What do we know?" I ask too excitedly. I know no one likes talking to me about Liesel's father. They all know that I think she's still alive, and no one has the heart to tell me differently.

"He's on a yacht." She doesn't say it excitedly. There's something she's not telling me.

"Where?" I move closer to her, getting in her face trying to read her mind and hesitation.

"Here. The yacht is less than ten miles away. He stole one of our ships and has been moving it around the Pacific Ocean, getting close occasionally, but not so close that we would suspect him. Until now."

"It's a trap?"

She nods. "He wants us to find him. That's what's changed."

Shit.

I stare out into the ocean. I can't see any yachts except for Kai and Enzo's, but he's here. He's been taunting us this entire time with how close he is—something's changed.

"What do we do?" she asks.

"We go kill him." And we find Liesel alive.

23

LIESEL

"BISHOP to the second white square from the right," I say.

"That's bishop to F5," Corbin sighs, exacerbated with me for once again not using the actual names of the squares. In the months we've been playing chess with each other in our heads, I've learned what the squares are called, but I like annoying him.

"It doesn't matter what the name of the square is; that's check," I say.

"Actually, that's checkmate," Maxwell says, throwing a ball he made out of aluminum foil and catching it.

"It's not. It can't be," Corbin goes through the position of all my pieces in his head, trying to figure a way out of it. I don't think there is a way. My queen and bishop are positioned perfectly, and I have his king stuck in a corner. I think I've won.

"Dammit," Corbin finally curses. "You win again."

I grin as I lay on my cold mattress with my arms behind my head, staring up at the ceiling.

"Your turn to play me, Max."

"Nope, I'm not playing chess with you. You know how much I hate using my brain that much."

"We could play checkers?"

"No."

"Tic-tac-toe?"

"No."

"Fine, push-up or pull-up challenge?"

"Push-ups," Max grins.

Corbin and I roll my eyes. While Corbin prefers to work his brain, Maxwell prefers to be entertained with games of physical strength.

We all roll off our mattresses to the floor. We get in position to start our push-ups, and then Maxwell shouts, "Go!"

We don't have a timer or any sort of clock to measure how many we can do in a set time. Instead, we just go until one of us can't anymore, then we count. In the months we've been doing this, I've only won the pushup contest once. And that was only because Maxwell was sick with a cold, and Corbin let me win.

I don't expect to win, but it is fun to watch the two brothers compete.

I move quickly, doing as many push-ups I can before I exhaust my arms. I love how it feels to have my blood pump fast, and my lungs burn with exertion.

I get lost in how my body feels. I forget my pain, how I've failed to kill my father. I forget about everything. If I'm honest, I think doing the physical games take my mind away from everything better than the mental games with Corbin. But I wouldn't ever tell Corbin that. Both brothers are trying their best to take care of me and distract me.

My arms continue to push my body up off the floor before lowering myself back down—again and again and again.

Finally, I collapse. My arms no longer have the strength to lift again.

The boys notice and stop their push-ups.

"One hundred and five," Corbin says.

"One hundred and thirteen," Maxwell says and then looks to me. "Liesel? Are you alright?"

I can tell by his voice that I don't look good. I'm sure my face is pale, my breathing shallow and erratic. "I've been waiting for death for a long time; it never comes. I'm not going to die because I did too many push-ups."

"Still, you should take it easy," Maxwell says.

"This is why we should play mental games, not physical ones," Corbin says.

I sit up to prove that I feel fine. "I'm fine. See, perfectly fine."

I feel my stomach twisting, and I suspect I'll be sick soon. I take a couple of slow breaths, trying to ease my queasiness. I try to hide how I feel from them, but they notice.

"Come here," Corbin says.

I inch myself closer to the bars on his side. He wets a cloth and presses it to my forehead before lifting a bottle of water to my lips.

"Drink."

I take a couple of small sips, but it's all I can stomach.

"How are you feeling?" Maxwell asks.

There's no use lying. "My stomach is burning and wants to eject everything inside it."

Corbin and Maxwell exchange worried looks.

I don't know how I'm still alive, honestly, except that I have unfinished business. My father is still alive; still a threat to my children and my body refuses to die until my father is dead.

Speaking of the devil, my father makes his almost daily appearance.

"You don't look so good, my daughter."

"I look better than you," I say, forcing my body up. I won't look weak in front of him. Just like my father won't look weak in front of me.

We both know the other is dying; we are both sick. We're playing a game of chicken, trying to appear braver and healthier than the other. My father thinks I can be saved. As soon as I do what he says, he thinks he can give me the drugs to save me. But if that were true, he'd use them on himself and live.

I don't know what his game is exactly. He knows I'm dying, that I can't take over for him, and yet he keeps trying. Every. Single. Day.

"Don't you have something better to do with your day than annoy us?" Corbin asks.

My father ignores him.

"Today is a very special day."

"The day you finally keel over dead?" Maxwell asks.

"It's been one year exactly. It's time to decide."

"Decide what?" I ask.

"Decide who I'm going to kill first—Rose or Atlas?"

I frown. Nervous energy zips through my body before I blow out a breath, letting the anxiety go. He can't get to Rose or Atlas. They are completely protected. I don't have to worry about him killing them.

"Neither."

"So confident in your beau to protect them. So stupid of you to think that I can't kill them."

"You can't," I say defiantly.

He pulls out his phone and starts a video. It's of Langston playing with the kids. I become transfixed by the video. They've all grown so much. Rose now towers over her two brothers. Declan has grown his hair out, while Atlas has gotten a recent buzzcut. They look happy, content, safe. My eyes drift to Langston. He's lost weight, but not muscle. His eyes are hollow and slightly red. I'm guessing from lack of sleep or excess alcohol.

I touch the screen with my fingers, wishing I could send him my love and comfort. I wish I could let him know that I'm alive, but that would break him. He's strong but in a fragile state. I won't be the reason he breaks.

The video ends, and I hand the phone back to my father. "This means nothing."

"It means I have a spy on the inside. Did you see the angle this video was taken from?"

"Who?" I can't believe anyone there would spy for my father. Not any of our friends. Not any of the employees.

"Phoenix."

I gasp.

"Phoenix wouldn't risk the kids' lives. She loves them," Maxwell says.

I agree. She would never hurt them.

"Maybe, but then she would do anything to save her brothers' lives."

"You bastard! I'm going to kill you," Corbin says.

My father smirks. "I'm going to win. The sooner you realize that, the better. There is no use in you rotting your life away in this cell."

"Just because you got Phoenix to take a video for you doesn't mean she'll help you get to one of the kids. You won't get anywhere near the island."

"Oh, child, how you underestimate me. Where do you think we are?"

He pulls up another video. This one is a security feed from the yacht we're on, apparently. It's staring straight ahead at Langston's island.

He turns the phone off and then turns, walking to my cell door. He pauses.

"You have until midnight to decide which child dies."

I squeeze my eyes shut. I can't take the chance that he could get his hands on one of my kids. I have no doubt if he got close, he'd kill one of them. He doesn't need all three as a backup. He just needs one.

"Wait!" I scream.

My father stops.

"What do you want me to do?"

24

LIESEL

"KILL HIM," my father says.

"I would, except you won't let me out of this cell, and he's too smart for you to catch." I'm not sure if that's true. Phoenix may easily give Langston over in exchange for her brothers getting to live. She'd definitely prefer to hand over Langston than one of the kids.

"The time will come when you will have the opportunity to kill Langston. Until then, in order for me to not head to the island tonight to kill one of your children, prove that you've stopped loving Langston."

"How?" I ask, even though I know I'm going to regret asking.

A sly grin forms on his vile face as he looks from Corbin to Maxwell. "Have your pick."

"Fuck one of them, you mean."

"Yes, fuck them, want them. Show me you've forgotten all about that stupid boy. Show me you're strong enough to do what it takes to be a leader."

I take a deep breath. Fucking another man doesn't mean

that I've stopped loving Langston. He would understand and forgive me for cheating. He has before.

I look at Corbin and Maxwell out of the corner of each eye. They are frozen in place, trying to figure out how to kill this devil. Maybe this is our chance. He hasn't let us out of these cells in a year. This might be our first opportunity.

"I assume if I do this, you'll at least allow me a proper bed. I'm not fucking either of them in this dark cell."

"That can be arranged."

"So what? I fuck one of them, and you don't kill any of my children? Then you throw us back in these cells?"

"Afterwards, I'll decide if you still love Langston or not. If you do, you'll go back in this cell to think about it for another year. If you don't, then we can start your transition to power and go after him together."

This is my chance. He'll take us upstairs. We will be out of these cells. We could find a way to kill him tonight. Or, at least, I could convince him I don't love Langston anymore and be free of this cell, giving me plenty of more time to kill him. Worst case, we end up back in these cells without succeeding.

We have to succeed. I won't survive another year.

"I'll arrange for you to be brought out of your cell in an hour. You can choose which of your cellmates you'd prefer to seduce then."

"What if I want to fuck them both?"

"If that's what you choose, then fine."

His eyes warn me, knowing why I asked. They're both on my side, and I want to improve our odds of defeating my father.

"You have one hour." He closes my door and looks from me to Corbin, then to Maxwell. "Plan well. You're only going to get this one chance to kill me. You don't want to know what's going to happen when you fail."

His words are a warning. If we make an attempt on his life and fail, he'll kill one of us.

He'll kill Corbin or Maxwell.

We can't fail.

———

After my father leaves, the three of us stare at each other. None of us know what to do. We can't discuss a plan together—my father would listen in on the security cameras.

Instead, we sit quietly by ourselves, contemplating our plans. I try to go through all the possibilities. I try to come up with anything I can use as a weapon. All the tricks Langston taught me about how to get out of bindings, how to protect myself, I think of it all.

I don't know how fast or slow time moves. Since we've been locked up, time has been a strange element. We never know when it's day or night. It's hard to even keep track of the days when you have no sun to count, nor work or activity to mark the difference between days.

This hour passes in much the same—both slowly and all at once.

Corbin, Maxwell, and I exchange reassuring glances as we hear the approach of footsteps nearing the door that leads to our cells. We don't have to talk to know that we have a plan. We are going to succeed. We are going to kill my father. We might not all survive, but that isn't the goal. The goal is to put an end to this. Any sacrifice any of us make will be worth it.

We all stand and face the doors of our cells, ready to fight no matter what comes.

Suddenly, my world goes dark.

———

I open my eyes, and the room is bright—so fucking bright that I immediately close them again, but not before I get a glimpse of Corbin standing over me.

"Where are we? The surface of the sun?" I ask.

He chuckles.

"No, we're in a room above deck with windows. That's the first ray of sunshine you've seen in a year."

I flutter my eyes, trying to open them, but honestly, I prefer the dark.

"Here," Maxwell says.

A second later, the blinds are blocking the light enough for me to open my eyes.

"Better?" Maxwell asks.

I nod and then sit up.

It makes me immediately queasy. Corbin notices the familiar motion and grabs a trash can for me just in time as the contents of my stomach come up.

"What happened?" I ask after my stomach stops heaving.

"He drugged you before he even entered your cell."

"Just me?"

Corbin nods. "Yea, he didn't have to drug us. He knew once he had you, we would do whatever he said. He brought us all into this room and then left. He hasn't spoken to us yet. Our best guess is you've been out for about an hour."

"Have you found any way out?" I ask, even though I know they can't answer me, at least not with words.

We did come up with signals for yes and no in situations like this to answer basic questions without my father or his men seeing what our real answers are.

"No," Corbin says.

He grabs my hand and helps me stand up off the couch I was lying on. He squeezes my hand twice before letting it go.

Our signal for yes was to make any motion twice, a single time for no.

Twice for yes.

They've found a way out of here.

The problem is they can't communicate it to me, so I just have to follow their lead of when or how to get out of here.

I look around the room. It's half living area, half bedroom. There is a couch I was lying on and two chairs. Then there is a large king-sized bed on the other side.

I gulp at the sight. I don't know if their plan of escape involves doing what my father wants before or after we use the bed.

I pace around the room as the two men's eyes are locked on me. I take in the two large windows that are now covered with blinds. I run my hand over the edge of the bed, the couch, the chairs, the door, the walls. I study the cameras I can see and guess where there could be more that I can't see.

I jump when I hear my father's voice.

"Prove to me that you don't love him anymore. Commit one of the worst sins."

And then his voice is gone.

I feel the two men behind me, and I know what I must do —fuck them like I want them.

There was a time when I would have been capable of this, even while loving Langston. But without seeing Langston for over a year, I'm not sure I'm strong enough. My heart longs for Langston so strongly that I'm not sure I can even go through the motions with someone else, let alone convince my father.

I don't turn around. I can't face Maxwell and Corbin. They've become friends, practically brothers in our year together.

"I can't," I whisper, letting them know I'm going to need all the help I can get.

I hear both men walk to me, stopping on either side of me.

They each take one of my hands and squeeze twice.

Yes.

I don't know what they are trying to say yes to; just that is the signal they are giving me.

"Close your eyes," Corbin says.

I do.

"Take a deep breath and let go of everything. Let your mind drift to what you want it to," Maxwell says.

And then I feel a blindfold placed over my eyes.

I gulp for air, like losing my sight also affected my ability to breathe.

They lead me over to the bed until the backs of my thighs graze the edge. A hand on my shoulder lowers me to the bed. I sit, but I don't fall back.

"Picture him, not us."

I can't tell if that was Maxwell or Corbin who said that.

I don't know how I'm supposed to show that I'm over Langston if they had to blindfold me for me to fuck them.

"It won't work."

"Trust us. It will."

Picture Langston.

Pretend it's Langston.

My memories of the last time we were together are so foggy that I can barely remember. *What did it feel like to have his lips pressed against mine? Were they soft and sweet? Hard and controlling? Would I lose my breath, or would my heart rate speed? Was I overcome with emotion, or so lost in him that I felt no emotion at all?*

I can't remember.

I've been living without him for so long that I've forgotten all of the little details. *What shade was his hair up close? Was his smile crooked or straight?*

Hands gently glide me down until I'm lying on my back.

I purse my lips and let out a slow, calming breath.

Maxwell and Corbin aren't going to hurt me. They are just doing what is necessary for us to protect my kids and kill my father.

"Think of him," Corbin says. Then I feel warm, wet lips against mine.

The kiss takes my breath away. I wasn't expecting anything so intimate from either of them. Fucking yes, kissing no.

"Him."

The lips don't leave mine. I don't know if it's Corbin or Maxwell kissing me, but he's persistent in his drive to get my lips to part.

Think of Langston. Think of the man I've been so desperate to forget because thinking of him was too painful.

Finally, I open my lips.

His tongue takes full advantage, dipping into my mouth and controlling every part of it. It sweeps over my tongue, pulling a low moan out of me.

My body comes alive again. I never thought I'd be here, writhing under Langston again, but I am.

His hardness is hovering over my body but isn't pressed against me like I want. I tug on his bottom lip with my teeth, encouraging him to come closer.

I hear moaning, but it's not his.

It's Corbin or Maxwell, but somehow it feels distant, not close.

It's because I'm imagining Langston, not them. My mind is playing tricks on me, pushing their voices out, but I can't quite invent Langston's voice out of thin air, not when I haven't heard his deep timbre in so long.

I don't need to imagine his voice. Whoever is kissing me is doing plenty to stir my memories of Langston. I remember how his kisses would start off by taunting me, making me feel like I'm in control before demanding everything from me. I'd feel his kisses to the deepest parts of my core and all the way to the tip of my toes—it's how I feel now.

I grab for his shirt and yank him to me.

His body fits perfectly over mine.

How can a man who isn't Langston fit so well with my body? Is it Maxwell or Corbin?

No.

This is Langston.

Langston!

I let my fantasy of the man touching me being Langston fill my head. I won't think of Maxwell or Corbin again.

He pushes my shirt up my body as he kisses my stomach then up to the curve of my breasts. He pulls the shirt off my body, so he can stare at my body unobstructed. He pauses, not touching me, kissing me, or whispering dirty thoughts. He must be doing nothing but looking at me.

I bite my lip as I feel a blush come over me. *Does he not find me attractive anymore?* I know I've been through hell. My body is weak, bruised, scarred. I don't have the curves I used to.

It's been so long since we've fucked that I'm sure he no longer finds me attractive.

"Maybe you should wear a blindfold too and imagine someone else," I whisper.

He catches my wrist as I try to push him away and kisses the tender spot of my palm.

I can't help but moan at the softness of his lips. Then his lips are at my ear.

I shiver from the hotness of his breath building pleasure through my body.

"I can't take my eyes off you," he says.

My breath catches. His voice sounds like what I

remember Langston's to be. My mind is fully committed to the fantasy.

He starts kissing down my body again, not missing a single inch of skin. I get lost in the pleasure. With my blindfold on and not feeling anything like this in a year, my body is tingling everywhere his lips press. So much so that I don't notice that he's removed my pants until I feel him kiss between my legs.

I gasp loudly—so loudly that he stops to check that I'm okay. He continues when he realizes it's just because the intensity of his touch is overwhelming me, not hurting me.

My body is torn between indulging in the feel of his hot lips between my legs and knowing how wrong this is. A tingle of fear simmers under the surface. *What if my body no longer knows how to do this? What if it hurts?*

My thighs squeeze against the sides of his head as his tongue slides up my slit. It's exactly the same way Langston used to lick me.

Waves of pleasure ripple through my body. His hands push at my thighs until they fall open for him, giving him complete access to my body.

I'm going to hell for enjoying this.

His tongue swirls around my clit, and I completely let go.

"Fuck!" I moan as I feel my orgasm climbing in record time. I've never come so fast.

The sensations and feelings overwhelm me. I lose all thoughts. I lose all sense of what I'm supposed to be doing. I can't help myself.

I moan loudly. "Yes, just like that! I'm coming. Lang—"

A hand covers my mouth, muffling my screams.

LANGSTON

I WANT nothing more than to hear Liesel screaming my name as I fuck her. I don't know Corbin and Maxwell's exact plan, but I do know that her screaming my name right now is the opposite of helpful. I muffle her screams with my hand and then eventually my mouth.

I don't think she realizes that it is actually me who is kissing her, touching her, making her come. The reason her body is so responsive is because I'm the one fucking her.

Liesel is wearing a blindfold. She's not privy to Corbin and Maxwell's plan, although I'm not much either. I think they are afraid if she sees me, her reaction will give away my presence.

I snuck onto the yacht and into this room, realizing it was where Mr. Dunn was bringing them. I'm outnumbered by myself on this boat. If I were smart, I would've brought Enzo, Beckett, or Zeke, but I need to do this on my own. I need my own hands wrapped around Liesel's father's neck.

I've been hiding under the bed so the security cameras wouldn't spot me. It was almost impossible to stay hidden when Liesel's limp body was first brought into the room, but then I watched Corbin and Maxwell take care of her. They studied the room and tried to come up with a plan wordlessly. I knew they had a plan even though they didn't speak it out loud.

My heart raced when I heard her father's words, when I knew what she had to do.

I almost gave away my hiding spot when they blindfolded her and led her to the bed. I thought they were going to go through with it with me hiding under the bed.

I was just about to reveal myself when the lights flickered, and the electricity went out.

Maxwell crouched under the bed with a finger to his lips, telling me to be quiet, while motioning for me to come out.

So I did.

We all stared at Liesel sitting on the bed, scared out of her mind. Both men nodded at me to approach her.

It took every ounce of control in me not to lift her up in my arms and carry her away, but I put my trust in the two brothers who have kept her safe for over a year.

It didn't take me long to realize they had somehow fucked with the visual aspect of the security cameras, but not the audio.

They started moaning and making grunting sounds that were hilarious to watch and listen to. I realized my task was to make Liesel make sounds to match theirs.

If this is how I save Liesel, how I save us all, by making her orgasm, by fucking her—I can't think of a more enjoyable way to save us.

"My turn," Maxwell shouts.

They're standing near the door with their backs to us. They're trying to stall until they figure a way out of here. I don't know if we are going to live or die, but either way, I need Liesel more than I need air right now.

I don't move from Liesel. I don't want to think she's

being shared. I want to tell her it's me, but I'm not sure what her reaction will be. And I'm having a hard enough time keeping her moaning and not shouting my name as it is. If she knows it's me for sure, it's going to be that much harder.

Plus, I enjoy watching her body respond to me even though she thinks it's not me. It's like we are fucking again for the first time. I have to convince her all over again that she wants me, remind her that she craves me.

As much as I want to feel her skin against my skin, I decide it's best to keep as many of my clothes on as possible in case I have to make a quick escape.

I notice Maxwell and Corbin are doing jumping jacks and push-ups and have removed half their clothes to make it seem like they were the ones who fucked her, not me.

Now, to actually fuck her, so her father has proof that she doesn't love me.

Liesel is still breathing hard as I lower my lips to hers. I kiss her as slowly as I can manage, but after missing her for a year, unsure if she was alive or dead, it's near impossible. It's especially difficult with the sounds she's making when I kiss her—soft, delectable moans.

I have to remember to let her moans escape my lips so they can be heard on the cameras. But damn, do I want to capture them all for myself.

She writhes beneath me as I press my body against hers.

"Why do I want you so much?" she asks.

Because you love me.

I tease her nipple with my fingers, squeezing it and making her arch her back into me.

"I'm sorry, Langston. I'm sorry, but I want you, whoever you are," she says.

I let her words out because they'll help convince Liesel's father that she's falling for whichever man is supposed to be fucking her.

But she has nothing to be sorry for. I know that if Corbin or Maxwell were really the ones trying to fuck her, she would be different. She doesn't want them like she wants me.

I consider telling her, but we need to keep the charade up longer. She can be a good actress when she wants to be, but I suspect seeing me again will end in a fountain of tears. It will take too long for her to compose herself to make the sounds she needs to make. So I make her endure for a little longer.

At least I can make her body feel good in the process.

I move back to her ear. "Trust me," I whisper, knowing that her mind isn't processing my words correctly. She doesn't recognize it's me.

I rub her clit to ensure she's as wet as possible. She's ready for me, but despite that, I don't want this to hurt for a second. I don't want her afraid.

I pull my cock out and ease it against her entrance.

She stiffens. Her thighs clamp shut while wetness oozes onto my cock. She's conflicted. Her body wants this, but her brain is telling her to stop.

Corbin and Maxwell notice her hesitation.

They walk over with their backs to us.

"Do you want me?" Corbin asks.

Liesel holds her breath like she doesn't want to answer.

"What about when I do this?" he asks.

I circle her cit then squeeze it.

She moans so loudly I'm sure the entire ship can hear her.

I stop.

"No, don't stop," she moans.

I slide my cock back to her slit as I continue to rub her clit, not letting up the pace this time as I ease her into the idea of letting me fuck her. But even with how riled up her body is, I can still sense her hesitation.

Corbin starts to speak again, and I take it as my opportunity to speak without being heard.

"I love you, huntress," I whisper.

She gasps, finally recognizing my voice. Her legs part immediately, and her body welcomes my cock in.

I bite my own lip to stifle my moan as Corbin groans loudly, pretending it's him instead of me. It's going to be impossible for me to keep my moans to myself when being inside her feels like heaven. She's wrapped around me so tightly that if I move, I'll come, so I don't dare move.

But Liesel is desperate for more of me. She rocks her hips, and I groan louder.

Corbin covers my groans with his, but I can't chance them hearing another voice on the recording.

I plant my lips on hers. "Don't stop kissing me."

She doesn't.

Now that she knows it's me, she devours me. Her kisses are frantic, hungry weapons she uses to put me at her mercy for making her think she was fucking another man. Her hands tangle in my hair as I sink deeper into her body.

Everything disappears except her and me.

We float away on a cloud, all the pain of the last year, of our lifetime, disappears. This time, there is nothing that will rip us apart. This time, we are going to last forever.

That's what I try to tell her with every thrust. It's what she agrees to with every rock of her hips.

I feel us both so close to orgasm. My body trembles over her, trying to drag this out as long as I can. Her lips suction to mine, trying to keep me silent as she moans around them.

I hope to hell Corbin and Maxwell have a plan because I know as soon as I finish, her father will burst through the door to look for proof of what he heard but couldn't see.

I look at Corbin out of the corner of my eye. He nods, letting me know he's ready.

Then I spend my last seconds enjoying Liesel before the battle begins. But this time, we are going to battle together, and we're going to win.

I drive hard into Liesel, and she comes a second before I do. My lips stay pressed to hers, and I do everything I can to suppress my own groans while letting hers out.

Then before I know what's happening, Corbin rips me from her body and pushes me back under the bed.

LIESEL

I RIP THE BLINDFOLD OFF, so sure I'll find Langston on top of me. Instead, I find Corbin and Maxwell butt naked on either side of the bed next to me.

I frown.

Did I imagine Langston? I know I was trying to pretend, but there was no way my mind could so convincingly persuade me that I was fucking Langston if I wasn't.

Could it?

I stare at Corbin, then Maxwell, looking for clues of what happened. From the obvious evidence, it looks like they fucked me, and I imagined Langston. Both are covered in sweat and the smell of sex. Both are naked. Both are here while Langston isn't.

They must have fucked me, not Langston.

But his words...*I love you, huntress.*

Did I dream up those words?

Did I so badly want Langston to be here that I convinced myself he was?

The door bursts open, and my father steps inside.

Both Corbin and Maxwell move protectively in front of me, blocking my naked body from my father's peering eyes.

He studies the scene and then must come to the same conclusion that I did. "You did well."

He walks over to a door at the back of the room and unlocks it. "There's a shower and a change of clothes inside. You boys can clean up in there."

He tosses a robe in our direction. "Liesel and I need to have a chat about what we are going to do about Langston."

Maxwell hands me the robe, and I slip it on. I'm hesitant to leave alone with my father, but this is our chance. We all feel the shift in the air. I'll go with him. If the opportunity presents itself, I'll kill him.

In the meantime, they will break out of this room and come for my father if I don't succeed. This room isn't as secure as the cells were.

I stand in the fluffy robe, and I smile at both men, hoping they can read my thoughts. They tense protectively as I stand off the bed and walk toward my waiting father.

I should be thinking about how I'm going to kill him. Instead, all I can think about is that I fucked Corbin and Maxwell, and I enjoyed it. I'm going to hell. I hate that I betrayed Langston.

My father exits the room, and when I turn to follow him, something catches my eye, making me turn back—the slightest movement under the bed.

Was it a mouse?

Golden eyes are staring back at me with a smirk. He lifts a finger to his lips, reminding me to be quiet.

I didn't imagine him. *Langston is here.* I have no doubt he was the one who fucked me. I didn't betray him, not again. It was him this whole time.

My heart soars, but I'm also terrified that he's here. His being here makes my father's task of killing him easier, and it makes my task of eventually saying goodbye to Langston harder.

I force myself to stop staring at the only man I've ever loved and turn to follow my father.

None of them will have trouble breaking out of this room, but as I shut the door, I leave it cracked just the slightest, ensuring they can escape. Finally, I follow my father. I know what I have to do.

I just hope that Corbin keeps his promise.

THE DOOR SHUTS, and I scramble out from under the bed.

"Thank god you showed up when you did," Maxwell says, pulling me in for a hug even though he's still naked.

"I'm sure Corbin would have found a way to do what had to be done. He's done it before," I growl.

Corbin winces. "I deserve that, but things have changed. She's like a sister to me now. We've spent a year sharing a cell next to each other. It would have been hard to hurt her like that."

"Is that what's happened this last year? You were all locked up in a cell?" I ask, afraid of their answers.

"Yes, we've been locked up in a cell on this yacht for a year. We haven't been let out or seen the sun for a year. That's how long he gave Liesel to change her mind about you. If she didn't, he'd kill one of her children."

"I'm going to kill him," I growl.

"That's the plan," Maxwell chuckles.

Corbin walks into the bathroom and finds the change of clothes. They start getting dressed without showering. We don't have time to waste.

"You did a good job with your grunting and moaning. You convinced him at least," I say.

"Well, we had to grunt so loudly because someone couldn't stop groaning," Maxwell teases.

"It's been a year; what did you expect?"

He chuckles.

"What's the plan?" I ask.

"Do you have a gun?" Corbin asks.

I pull out my gun and two knives, which I toss in their direction. They each catch a knife, ready to fight.

"We need to figure a way out of here. I'm not sure about the door. It looks like it's been reinforced. We might have to try one of the windows," Corbin says.

I nod.

"Then we take any weapons we can from the guards, find Liesel and her father, and kill him. If we can't find him, we'll pretend we've captured you and are bringing you to him."

I nod, recognizing the start backup plan of pretending to be their prisoner.

Corbin and Maxwell go to the windows while I see if I can break out through the door. There's a crack of light shining between the door and the frame. I push, and the door pops open.

"Guys, this way!"

Corbin and Maxwell run toward me.

"How'd you get it open?" Maxwell asks.

"Liesel left it open," I say.

"She's going to kill him long before we get there," Corbin says.

I grin. "I know, but she's going to get our help whether she needs it or not."

28

LIESEL

"Where are we going?" I ask.

"Somewhere where we can be alone."

I squeeze the robe tighter around my body as I follow my father to the furthest end of the yacht. I don't know how long it will take the men to follow us. I hope they are already behind us, watching where we're going.

We reach the back of the yacht, and then my father motions for me to climb down a ladder leading to a smaller boat.

This is a trap.

Perhaps the only reason I'm wearing a robe is so he knows I'm not hiding a gun. Thankfully, I don't need a weapon to kill him.

I want to ask again where we're going, but it doesn't matter. Everyone I love is safe. This is between my father and me.

I climb down onto the small boat. My father climbs down after me. He unties the boat and starts the motor. Then we're zipping across the water. I stare out at the unknown ocean instead of the yacht and men we just left behind. They can't save me now. I'm on my own.

My father knows, I realize.

He knows Langston is on the yacht.

He knows Corbin and Maxwell are planning to take him down.

He knows I didn't really betray Langston; I still love him.

Suddenly, my father shuts the engine off, and we're floating in the middle of open water. The yacht is no longer in sight behind us, and the island isn't visible either.

"You brought me here to kill me," I say, not looking at my father.

I try to figure out what my options are, but I prefer it this way—just him and me.

He doesn't answer, but then I guess I didn't really ask him a question.

I turn and face him. He doesn't move. He doesn't speak. He just stares at me with a blank expression.

I feel a cool breeze on my face and notice dark clouds stirring behind my father. We're going to get caught in a storm. I want to be the one to kill my father, but if I don't succeed, then I'd be happy for the storm to take my father's life.

"You can't kill me," I say.

"No, but I can make your life hell, so you'll wish you were dead."

"You're dying. I can see the gauntness in your eyes, the paleness of your skin, your lost weight—you're dying. And you need a successor, or everything you've spent your whole life working for will be for nothing."

"You think I'm a cruel man, don't you, Liesel? I'm a monster who left you and your mother when you were a child. I shirked my responsibilities to become a mob boss for money and power. You think I kill for the thrill of it."

"Don't you?"

"No, I was just taught an important lesson early in life—love always fails. It's the cruelest monster alive."

"I agree; falling in love is incredibly cruel. But it's too late to stop me from suffering the hardships of love."

"I know. I failed. I should have stepped in sooner."

"Why do you want me to take over for you when you're gone? Why does it have to be a family member? Couldn't your second in command take over for you? Then you could leave my family and me alone."

"I've tried that. I took some time off when I was first diagnosed with cancer and let my second lead." He stares off into the ocean. "I lost twenty men. More than I've lost in a decade, he lost in less than a month. He didn't understand his responsibility to the organization, not just himself and power. You understand that, though. It's why you agreed to come out here with me by yourself, instead of risking your friends or lover's life. You'd rather risk your own life than those you love.

"I think I've been going about this the wrong way. The way to get you to take over for me when I'm gone is not to get you to stop loving, but to get you to love my men, my world, as much as I do."

"I'll never love ruining people's lives for profit. I will never love stealing from them, selling them addictive drugs that will eventually kill them, or selling people like property. I will never love being a monster like you."

"Then it seems we are at an impasse."

"It seems we are," I agree.

"You think you're dying from your own illness; or you think I'm going to be the death of you. I can see you're prepared to die, but you don't realize love is going to be what kills you. Love makes you weak, dependent, selfish. You'll do things you wouldn't otherwise do because you fell in love. Let me help you, teach you, and you can learn to be the greatest—"

The roar of an engine interrupts him.

He squints his eyes in the sound's direction. I don't have to turn around to know who is coming toward us. I'm running out of time to kill my father before I'm risking Langston, Corbin, and Maxwell's lives too.

I see my father reach for something, assuming it's a gun.

It's not.

It's worse.

I jump, but I'm not sure I'm going to be able to save them. I'm not sure I'm going to be able to save any of us.

29

LANGSTON

I HOLD my hands behind my back, pretending they are tied together, while Corbin and Maxwell pretend to be my captors.

We make our way quickly down the hallway until one of the guards walks toward us.

"We found him trying to break into Liesel's room. Where is Mr. Dunn?" Corbin asks the man.

The man frowns, looking at us suspiciously. He can't make sense of the situation, and I doubt he'll give us any answers, so I shoot him. Luckily I came prepared to be stealthy with my gun's silencer.

"Well, that was effective," Corbin says, reaching down to grab the man's gun.

"We need to hurry; I don't trust Dunn with Liesel for a second longer than necessary," I say.

I move to the front now that two of us have guns. Corbin follows with Maxwell, holding only a knife, trailing him.

I practically run down the hallway and up to the top deck, looking for Liesel. I see two more guards and shoot them both before they even notice us. Maxwell collects one of their guns, and then we split up, all searching for Liesel and her father.

Five minutes later, we are all huffing as we meet back on the top deck.

"I found nothing," I say.

Both Corbin and Maxwell shake their heads.

"Where could they have gone?" Maxwell asks.

I run to the railing of the yacht and look down. "One of the lifeboats is gone. Let's go."

I run down the stairs with Corbin and Maxwell following me. Thankfully there are two lifeboats on either side of the yacht. We can still find them; although, we have no idea which direction they went. They also could have hopped on a bigger, faster ship. They could have gone to land and be driving on the island. They could have gotten on a helicopter. They could already be long gone.

I try not to think about that.

We'll find her.

We have to.

We all jump on the small boat.

"Which way?" Corbin asks at the back. He'll be the one driving the boat.

I look in each direction. There is no obvious way to go, but my heart is pulling me west.

"This way," I point in the direction of the setting sun.

We take off. Each of us holds our gun at our side, ready to fight for a girl who has won our hearts. Before, I might not have believed they were on my side, but after everything that has happened, they are at least on Liesel's side.

"There they are!" Maxwell shouts from the front of the boat.

We all turn, and in the far off distance is their boat, floating in the middle of the sea.

"Hurry!" I shout back to Corbin.

"We're going as fast as this thing goes!" he shouts back.

Jesus, it's going to take forever to reach them.

There is nothing else to do but hope we get to them before he threatens her life. We are so close, and yet we can't protect her from here. We have to get closer.

I squint my eyes, trying to get a good view of what's happening, but I can barely make out their bodies sitting on the boat.

Liesel jumps.

Not off the boat like I want her to, but she tackles her father.

None of us speak as we speed as fast and as close as we can.

We all raise our guns, ready to take aim the second we can.

We watch in horror as Liesel battles her father.

She punches him hard in the face, knocking him out.

I breathe a sigh of relief.

Then, she does the craziest thing. She starts up the boat, but instead of driving it toward us, she drives it away.

"What is she doing?" Maxwell asks.

"No clue; follow her," I tell Corbin.

Our boat must be faster than hers, or she isn't driving at full speed because we are catching up to her.

"I'm going to jump," Maxwell says as the tip of our boat comes along the side of the back of hers.

He jumps onto her boat successfully. I move up to jump onto her boat as well when Liesel's eyes catch mine. She turns her boat sharply, and we speed past her.

"Liesel!" I yell, confused by her actions.

"Max will help her steer in the right direction," Corbin says.

I don't think she's having problems steering. I think she's doing it on purpose, but I don't tell Corbin that.

"Just get us back to her boat," I yell.

Corbin sharply course corrects our boat.

Maxwell furiously grabs Liesel.

"What the hell is he doing?" I ask, terrified that he's hurting her as she kicks and screams in his arms.

Corbin doesn't answer me. It's clear he isn't sure either. We are definitely missing something, but I don't know what.

He drops her into the sea as she screams something back at him.

Then he grabs the engine's controls, and the boat speeds off away from us.

"Liesel," I yell as we approach her, floating in the ocean.

I dive into the water and swim toward her just as her head comes up out of the water.

I wrap my arms around her, never feeling safer than I am now. I'm never letting her go again—never.

"You have to stop Maxwell. My father started a bomb. I couldn't diffuse it. It's got less than a minute before it explodes," she cries into my arms.

"Shit."

Corbin pulls up next to us, and I quickly help her onto the boat before I pull myself up.

"Maxwell! Jump!" I yell, hoping he'll hear me and jump. It's his only chance.

We won't make it to him in time. We can't get any closer without risking the bomb killing us all, either.

Maxwell turns and looks at Corbin before jumping into the ocean. He hits the water just as the bomb goes off.

Liesel shrieks.

Corbin freezes.

I close my eyes, unable to handle the most likely outcome.

I turn to Liesel, who looks the more stable out of the two of them. "Stay here until I tell you it's safe to come closer."

She nods, and then I kiss her on her lips. One passionate kiss to hold us over, but it won't be the last. I dive into the water to swim closer, hoping to find Maxwell alive and her father dead.

The boat has been blown into a million pieces. I have no doubt that her father was planning on tossing the bomb onto our boat at the last second. Instead, his own need to control his daughter's life led to his death.

I see blood and pieces of his body floating in the water, and relief of his death washes over me.

"Maxwell!" I shout when I see his head bobbing up and down.

I swim as hard and as fast as I can in his direction. His head sinks below the water's surface.

"Dammit, Maxwell, why did you have to be a savior?" I mutter to myself as I dive down and push him up out of the water.

I know before I pull his head up that he's gone.

I feel my tears fall instantly.

For him.

For Liesel.

For Corbin.

He saved us all.

"Thank you, Maxwell. You saved her. You told me you would do anything for her. Thank you for keeping your promise," I say.

I squeeze my eyes shut as I hold his limp body. Corbin and Liesel are going to lose it when they realize he's dead. They must have all grown close being locked up in a cell together for a year—relying on each other, protecting each other.

All I want to do is heal. To become a family again. To put this horrible past behind us. But there is no easy way to heal after losing what we've lost.

Corbin eases the boat close enough for me to hear him, but not so close that they can get a clear view of Maxwell. It's probably for the best.

"Is he...?" Liesel asks.

"They're both gone," I answer.

She collapses down on the boat. I want nothing more than to wrap her in my arms and take away her pain, but I need to figure out what to do with Maxwell's body.

I look to Corbin for guidance. *Does he want his brother buried at sea? Or does he want to bring his body back to be buried somewhere?*

Corbin gives me a stern look I don't understand. He aims his gun at Liesel.

"No!" I shout.

Instead of shooting her, Corbin speeds off away from me.

"Liesel!" I shout, letting go of Maxwell and starting to swim after them.

Grief makes people do crazy things, but I have no idea what the hell Corbin is doing. And I definitely didn't fight so hard to get Liesel back just to lose her all over again.

LIESEL

As soon as we are out of sight of Langston, Corbin lowers his gun.

"Are you sure?" Corbin asks.

I stare back at the sea where we both left people we love floating in the ocean. Maxwell didn't survive. Langston will, but he'll have to learn how to live without me once again.

"I'm sorry. It was supposed to be me who died, not Maxwell," I say through my tears.

Corbin stops the boat for a second and wraps his arms around me as we both sob. "No, don't be sorry. Maxwell loved you. He wanted to protect you at all costs. He protected us all. We can miss him but don't be sorry that he died instead of you. You saved him a year ago. Without you convincing your father to help him, he would have died then."

I nod. He's right, but it's still hard.

Corbin grabs my cheeks and forces me to look at him again. "Are. You. Sure?"

I squeeze my eyes shut, closing off my tears.

"Kidnap me, make Langston think you killed me. Put an

end to his suffering. I don't want him to keep loving me, to keep hurting, because of me."

Corbin kisses my forehead, and then he begins to drive the boat again, fulfilling his promise to me.

I can't save Langston from heartbreak and pain, but I can end his suffering. I can save him from months of agony. It's time for him to start healing, no matter how hard it is. Maybe then I'll be able to rest in peace.

LANGSTON

O**NE** W**EEK** Later

I don't know the truth from the lies, but I do know that Liesel isn't dead. Corbin tried to make me believe it. It was convincing. The pictures. The video. Payback for losing his brother is what he said.

A lie.

But why? I have no clue.

I've tracked him to Portugal. His cousin has some land here that he's staying at. He hasn't been using a credit card, nor his own passport—nothing that would allow me to track him electronically.

It didn't stop me, though.

I found him.

I searched every relation, friend, and person he's ever met until I found him. It was almost like he wanted to be found. He was doing just the bare minimum to hide, not enough to keep me away for more than a week.

I expect to be walking into some sort of a trap.

Yet, I didn't bring Zeke, or Enzo, or Kai, or Beckett, or Siren. I don't need backup to get Liesel back. I just need answers.

The mansion they are living in is gorgeous—three stories of beautiful curved arches with winding greenery and roses. A terrace overlooks a small vineyard for enjoying the wine grown here.

That's where I find them sitting on the terrace, drinking wine.

Liesel isn't dead.

And if she's his captive, he's treating her well. Although, if he's made her his sex slave, I guess he could be trying to convince her to like him. *Maybe she fell for him in their year together?*

No, she loves me.

If she loved him, she would have fucked him on the yacht, not me.

There is only one way to find out the truth.

I step out from the shadows.

"Spare any wine for me?" I fold my arms and lean against the side of the house.

Both Liesel and Corbin jump.

Corbin grabs his gun and aims it at Liesel.

"Move, and I'll kill her."

I scrunch my nose. "I thought you already did. Isn't that what the photos were supposed to convince me of?"

Corbin frowns and keeps the gun aimed at Liesel. I'm not really concerned with his actions. I'm worried about hers.

She hasn't moved, but her breathing hasn't sped either. She's not afraid for her life. There is no sign that he's tortured her. In fact, she looks better than she did a week ago. There's more color in her cheeks like she's been spending lots of time in the sun.

"Test me, and I'll make it a reality," Corbin says. *He's a good actor, but I don't believe him.*

"No, you won't."

"I will."

"No, you won't. I removed the bullets from your gun. You literally can't kill her."

He studies the gun before realizing I'm right.

I pull my gun out and aim it at him.

He freezes and looks at Liesel.

"Run, Liesel. I got this."

Prove my theories wrong, Liesel.

Run.

She doesn't run. She stands slowly and walks in front of Corbin. "Don't shoot him."

"Why?" I growl.

She doesn't answer, but she does step between Corbin and me.

"Why? He kidnapped you, faked your death. Why shouldn't I kill him?"

Break my heart, huntress. Tell me you love him.

"I told him to kidnap me."

I lower my gun. I don't want to threaten her life.

She looks away for a second. For a moment, I think she's looking at Corbin like she needs his assurance to tell me.

"I'm sorry," she starts. She doesn't have tears in her eyes, but I can tell whatever she's about to say is going to hurt me, possibly worse than anything she's ever told me before.

"I'll give you a moment to talk," Corbin says, sneaking away.

I don't give a shit about him. I don't care what he does. I care about her.

With Corbin gone, I close the space between us, but I don't dare make a move. Not until she speaks. Not until she breaks my heart.

"What's going on, huntress?"

One tear streaks down her cheek so fast I think I imagined it.

"I don't want to hurt you. I don't want to watch you in agony every day I'm alive. I can't."

I frown, not understanding.

I take her hands in mine. I can't help myself. I need to hold her in some way, even if she is leaving me for another man.

"You love him?" I ask.

She frowns into my eyes. "No—I mean, I love him like you love Siren. He's a close friend, nothing more."

"Then nothing you could say would break my heart."

She shakes her head.

"I'm dying."

"What?"

I look her up and down like I can somehow figure out what she's saying.

"I have colon cancer, and it spread. I don't have much time."

I pull her closer, not accepting her words.

"Atlas had cancer. I have cancer. And I'm pretty sure my father was also dying of cancer before the explosion. I think we have a hereditary gene that makes us all more susceptible. I've had it for a long time. It was in remission for a while, but in the last couple of years, it's come back. I don't know how I've lasted this long."

I wrap my arms around her and hold her firmly against my chest. I feel my tears welling, but somehow hearing that she has cancer and not that she doesn't love me is better. I can reverse cancer. I can't make her love me if she's in love with another man.

"Because you're the strongest person I know, that's how."

"I had Corbin kidnap me because I thought dying swiftly

186

would be easier for you than watching me die slowly and painfully. I can't watch your heart break again."

I grab her cheeks and peer into her eyes.

"Do you love me?"

"More than I should."

"Then my heart will never have to break."

"But—"

"No, I refuse to let you die. We've survived too much, you and I."

I kiss her, showing her how much I need her no matter what.

I know I can't control the world. I don't have any real power over whether she lives or dies, but I'm a stubborn bastard. And for however long I have left with her, I won't waste one second.

She moans into me.

I push her lips apart, dipping my tongue into her gasping mouth.

I grab her legs and wrap them around my waist as I carry her toward the house. I don't know if I can make it to a bed, but I don't want to fuck her on the deck.

She devours me with her mouth as I throw open the door and step inside. She's ripping my button-down shirt while my hand is frantically dipping beneath her sundress, feeling her moisture spread over her panties.

"Jesus, can you at least wait until I leave a room before you fuck her? I've seen you fuck more times than I need to," Corbin says as he starts to rush out of the room.

We chuckle into each other's mouths as we kiss.

"And Langston, you're welcome!" Corbin shouts as he jogs down the hall. "I'm sorry, Liesel!"

Liesel frowns. "The bastard. He was supposed to keep his word, so you didn't have to suffer."

I shake my head as I rub my cock between her legs as we

fall onto the couch. "No, I'll never suffer as long as I'm with you. You're wrong to think that you dying would somehow make my life easier."

I unzip my pants and ease my cock into her as she arches her back. Her eyes are hungry with need. She kisses me hard, which will make it hard for me to get the words out that I need to.

"I never wanted to love you. I tried for so long to not love you because I thought it would save you. In the end, it only cost me time with you. There was no way I couldn't fall for you," I say.

A tear brushes her cheek again.

I kiss it away.

"I never wanted to break your heart, but I've always loved you since you became my killer."

"I've loved you since I watched you hunt a spider and needed my help to kill it. But break my heart, huntress. Break it a thousand times if you must. Loving you will always be worth the heartbreak. Just promise me this—you'll let me love you for as long as we both have left. Love me as long as we are both living."

"I promise to love you and let you love me for as long as I live."

"I'll love you even when you're gone. But I don't accept that you'll be the first to die. I don't accept that either of us will die anytime soon. We have a lot of lost time your father cost us to make up for. Our forever won't end anytime soon."

And then I show her how much I love her by making love to her. Over and over and over. So loudly that we drive Corbin out of the big house.

She thinks this is the end of our story, that the end is near. We won't get our happily ever after.

Maybe she's right.

But I'm a believer that love can conquer all.

Our love is the greatest love story that's ever been told—call me biased.

Our story doesn't end with her slipping away in my arms before she turns thirty.

Our story is endless, and I'll fight every day to ensure it. We've fought the world before and won. *Why should this be any different?*

I look into her eyes; she doesn't believe me. It doesn't matter. Liesel may be right most of the time, but this time she's wrong. I'm right.

"Do you want to make a bet?" I ask.

She frowns. "A bet?"

"We are going to live happily ever after, for a very long time."

She smiles sadly. "What do I get if I'm right?"

"The ability to haunt my ass and ensure I'm never with another woman again."

It makes her laugh.

"And if I win, I get whatever I want. Deal?"

"Deal," she agrees.

"Good. I plan on winning."

She kisses me rather than continue our conversation, but when we are eighty and sitting in our rocking chairs together after living a long and happy life together, I'm going to collect on our bet.

FIRST EPILOGUE
LIESEL

ONE YEAR Later

"Mom!" Declan yells.

All three of my kids are running toward where Langston and I are lying on the beach.

They jump on me, ignoring their father.

"Why are you all jumping on me?" I ask as I laugh.

"Because Dad will say no," Rose says.

I laugh. She's probably right, but I have to hear this.

"Stop tickling me and tell me what you all want," I say, sitting up.

Langton is still lying still on the towel next to me; his cap draped over his eyes.

"The answer is no," Langston says without moving.

The kids jump at his voice.

Rose pouts.

Atlas smiles. "I told you he'd say no."

Declan rolls his eyes.

I look to each of my kids, one by one, seeing what it is

they want. As much as Langston pretends he can be a firm dad who tells his kids no, he can't. He'll cave. The kids know it; they just like to rile him up.

"Yes," I say.

"You don't even know what we are going to ask," Rose says.

"I'm your mother, so I already know what you're going to ask."

"We were going to ask to only ever eat ice cream for every meal for the rest of our lives," Atlas jokes.

I shake my head. "Nope."

"We were going to ask for millions and millions of dollars."

"Nope."

"You want to go visit Uncle Enzo, Aunt Kai, and the twins and go to Disney World with them," Langston groans.

"They did know," Rose says, her eyes bugging out that we would guess what our kids want.

I laugh.

"The answer is no," Langston says.

I bite back a smile. He knows I'm going to say yes, and he doesn't have a choice in the matter.

I know this.

The kids know this.

Langston knows this.

"How about you go get Dad a bowl of his favorite ice cream and see if it changes his mind?" I tell the kids.

All of their eyes light up. They run off, but not before I hear Rose say, "Mom's going to convince Dad to let us go. This is just a diversion, so we don't hear them argue. But just in case, we should bribe Dad with ice cream."

I lift Langston's hat off his face and am met with a scowl. Somehow I find him more attractive when he's angry than when he's smiling.

192

"Do we really have to take them to Disney World? That's the least safe place in the world."

I roll my eyes. "Yes, they're kids. They want to go to Disney World with their cousins."

"They live on a private island with their cousins; why do they need to go to Disney World?"

"We're going."

He frowns. "No, we're not. It's not safe."

I raise an eyebrow at him. "We aren't in danger. And even if we were, we aren't denying our kids the joys of the world."

"Disney World isn't a joy. It's a crowded, disease-infested, capitalistic hell."

"We're going."

"No—"

"I didn't survive a year longer than I should to not take our kids to Disney World with their cousins."

He frowns and grabs my hips, yanking me toward him so he can kiss me. "Fine, but you can't use the cancer card for another year."

I smile into his lips, knowing very well that I can and I will. Langston would do anything for our kids and me. We've built the perfect world here for them on this island, but that doesn't mean we are afraid to venture out into the real world.

Siren and Zeke finished their house here. Phoenix and Corbin live here as well. Rose and Atlas still call Phoenix 'Mom,' and it doesn't bother me in the slightest. I'm happy they can have two moms, a dad, and plenty of aunts and uncles who love them and would be willing to die to protect them.

Enzo and Kai live with their kids on their yacht and spend time between Miami and here, still leading their empire like the badasses they are.

Beckett stays with them a lot, but he's found a new girl in

Seattle who he's been spending a lot of time with. We're pretty sure he's in love, but we don't tell him that. We don't want to jinx his relationship. After all, all of our love stories put us through hell before we got to the happily ever after part.

SECOND EPILOGUE
LIESEL

Tᴇɴ Yᴇᴀʀꜱ Later

My heart freezes when we get letters in the mail addressed to each of the kids.

My father.

I recognize the handwriting—the same handwriting that was on the letter that Langston and I tore in half.

I show the letters to Langston.

He immediately tosses them all in the fireplace, burning them all.

My father's empire is dead.

We've ensured it.

The decent people who used to work for him now work for Kai and Enzo. The rest we either killed or they found their way to new crime organizations.

We're safe.

Our kids have grown up only knowing love and safety. Even Declan has forgotten about the horrors of his past. We've protected them well, and they are all ready to fly the nest. I can't wait to see what adventures the world holds for them.

I pour myself a cup of coffee, needing an afternoon pick me up.

"You know what today is?" Langston asks after he gets over his grumpiness at seeing the letters.

"What?"

"Ten years exactly since we made our bet. Do you admit that I was right yet?"

I've been cancer-free for eight of the ten. Langston took me to every doctor in the world until we found something that worked.

"Would I ever admit that you're right? I would never lose a bet so easily. You said forever. Ten years isn't forever," I tease.

He wraps his arms around me and kisses my neck. "I'm going to enjoy the next fifty years proving how right I am."

THIRD EPILOGUE
LIESEL

Fifty Years Later

Langston holds my hand as we sit on the sand, staring out at the sunset.

"I win our bet, right?" he asks.

I grin.

"Yes, you win. So what do I have to do to pay my debt?"

He kisses me. "You already have, by giving me our forever."

The End

Thank you so much for reading Langston & Liesel's story! I hope you enjoyed reading it as much as I enjoyed writing it!

If you haven't read Kai and Enzo's story yet, check out the first chapter...

FIRST CHAPTER OF TAKEN BY LIES
ENZO

Alcohol.

It can lower your inhibitions.

Transform you into somebody society accepts.

Make you relax enough to ask the hot girl at the end of the bar out on a date.

Alcohol has so much power.

The power to tempt me.

To take me away.

To make me forget.

It should be only an act of rebellion. An underage misdemeanor, done as much for attention as to feel the effects. That's all alcohol should represent. I'm only seventeen. Still a long ways from twenty-one, but alcohol has never been a healthy pastime.

As soon as I tasted the liquid, I knew it was a habit I would never give up.

Not because I'm an alcoholic. That's one thing I could never be, even when I drink in large quantities. Even when I need alcohol as much as I need to breathe.

I need it to forget.

I finish the last drop of the amber liquid in my glass. One drink isn't nearly enough for me to forget. If there were another way to erase my demons and slip me into amnesia, I would take it. But I've never found another option. This is my only option.

"Another round," I say to Zeke and Langston who are sitting in the corner booth with me. It's not a question, but a statement.

I need more, and they will both stay with me, drinking until my past is erased for another hour.

Slinking out from beneath the corner booth hidden in the shadows, I stand and cross the width of the room before climbing onto a stool at the bar. We have a waiter, but I don't have the patience to wait for her to realize we need more drinks.

I eye Blake behind the bar. He knows when he sees me to drop his other patrons and serve me immediately. His tip, along with his job, requires it. This is just another bar my family owns. It's nothing in the grand scheme of things — just a place for me to retreat to when necessary. And lately, I've found coming here on a daily basis is very necessary.

Blake spots me out of the corner of his eye. He politely ends his conversation with the flirty woman at the end of the bar and walks my way, before pouring me another glass of the finest bourbon we have. I reach for the glass he sat in front of me and wait while he continues to make drinks for my friends.

I lift the glass to my lips taking comfort in the fact that soon my nightmare will be over. My memory will be obliterated, at least until I have to meet with my father later today.

The door flies open, and a girl falls through. She stumbles once as she drops to her knees. But her cheeks don't flame with embarrassment. Instead, fear threatens her eyes as she scans behind her. As if, any second, the evil she is running from will find her.

She stands quickly and brushes herself off out of habit, not because she's dirty. Her skin is a light olive color, but it's impossible to know what ethnicity she is just from the coloring. We live in Miami; everyone is tan. But her skin hints at more than just spending too much time in the sun. Hers promises a past and culture far more intriguing.

Her legs are too skinny I realize as I soak up her body and ingrain it in my memory like I do with everything. My memory is flawless, and even if it wasn't, there is no way I would forget such a spark of beauty like her.

Her clothes are too big for her. Her blue jean shorts engulf too much of her legs. Her tank top hangs like a tent instead of showing the curves beneath it. Dark black hair hangs down her neck in thick waves hiding her face.

But then she flips her head back and blows the rest of her locks from her face. Gone is the fear. Gone is the clumsy girl. Gone is the awkward girl uncomfortable in her own skin. I even forget her clothes are two sizes too big.

She's transformed from meek girl to powerful woman with one toss of her hair. Her steps are bold and robust as she struts toward the bar, only taking her three steps to reach the edge.

She smiles at the bartender, and Blake floats over to her, as under her spell as I am. I don't know what she says as she whispers to Blake, but I know he will retrieve whatever drink she ordered without verifying her age. And I'm right. Blake slides a beer to her without glancing at her ID. An ID that would either be fake or show she isn't any older than I am.

Her age doesn't matter though. The way she looks at him with piercing greenish blue eyes and unending poise is enough to persuade him to risk his job for her.

Blake may be used to serving underage clients, but that's only because of me. I've never seen him serve anyone unassociated with me who's so clearly a minor.

The girl lifts the glass to her lips, and the foam sits on her upper lip as she drinks down the golden liquid like it is the only thing keeping her alive.

That I can understand.

I shouldn't approach her. I shouldn't think about her. I shouldn't invite more evil into her world when it's clear she running from enough herself. But I can't fight the pull. I'm not strong enough.

I leave the drinks Blake placed in front of me for Langston and Zeke. I only take my drink as I slide into the stool next to her.

Her gaze never leaves her drink as I move next to her. She doesn't realize the danger that has approached.

"What's an innocent creature like you doing in a bar like this?" I ask.

Her eyes roll gently in her head, but it's the only sign she heard me. Otherwise, I don't exist to her.

But I'm a patient man. I know she heard me, and I know she is uncomfortable with me sitting so close. She'll answer. If for no other reason than she's curious as to why I converged on her in the first place. She may not show any fear right now, but she's running from something. And the tension in her neck is enough for me to know she's terrified of me outing her and returning her to whatever she's trying to evade.

She doesn't know I would never stop her from escaping. It's a feeling I understand too well. I would never stop someone from feeling free, if only for a moment.

"I needed something to eat. There isn't anything but bars on this road for miles."

I frown. *Food? That's her excuse?*

She downs her drink, and before the last drop crosses her lips, Blake brings another bottle to replace the empty beer still in her hands.

I smirk. "It seems you need alcohol a lot more than you need food."

She shrugs. "Alcohol helps too."

"This bar doesn't serve any food. You are out of luck."

She nods. "I know." She still doesn't look at me as she speaks. It's like she's talking to a ghost. Like I don't exist to her.

"I could turn you in for underage drinking. My family is close to the cops in this town. I could have you arrested. A permanent mark on your record. But maybe that would help you. Get you somewhere safe and away from whoever you are running from."

My words finally get her attention. Her bright eyes, looking more green now than blue, finally fall on my dark orbs. Her pink lips purse, and I think she's going to yell at me or plead for me to do anything but call the cops. I expect her to beg or to dash out the door again running in fear.

"You won't turn me in, and even if you do, I don't fear the police."

My finger traces the rim of my drink instead of tracing the outline of her soft lips like I want.

"I'm not a nice man. My conscience will have no problem turning you in. I'll sleep just fine knowing I put you in jail for a night."

She licks her plump lips, and my patience teeters on the edge of a cliff. *Why the hell do I want to taste her lips?* She's just a girl. Just like all the rest of the girls I went to high school with.

I groan silently. She's not like other girls. I don't know much about her, but I know she is *nothing* like other girls.

Her bright eyes narrow into slits about to tear out my throat, and I think I finally unnerved her.

"You're not a man. You're just a boy. Just like I'm a girl, not a woman. You're not twenty-one any more than I am."

She inches closer until her face is a breath away from mine. Her lips so close I could easily take them into my mouth before she could react and stop me.

She nibbles on her bottom lip as if she knows that's exactly what I want to do.

"You may control the police, but right now, I control *you*. You won't dare call the police on me."

I exhale, my eyes squinting as I study this fascinating girl in front of me. I've never met someone who spoke so many truths and so many lies in one sentence. I lurk forward, and she stills, exhaling harsh breaths but refusing to back down.

I lick my own lip, and I watch as her bottom one trembles. Our gazes lock in a fierce battle. Neither of us will back down. I could take what I wanted without a fight from her because she refuses to show weakness. I would guess she's always this strong.

Her life is as much a struggle as mine. We would make quite a pair. But I'm afraid our lives aren't meant to do anything but intersect for a brief moment. She's here to give me a tiny sliver of entertainment. She's a distraction from my own hauntings.

Blake places a plate of burger and fries in front of the girl.

My eyes widen for less than a second, but it's long enough for her to take it as a win. She smiles as she leans back in her chair before turning to her plate of food.

"I guess you don't know everything about this bar, *boy*," she says before shoveling a fry into her mouth.

I can't help but grin at her. The way she says boy, it doesn't feel like an insult, even though that's how she meant it. It feels freeing to seem like a boy in her eyes instead of a man who has too many responsibilities. I'm not the only one she has under her spell. This bar doesn't serve food, but it didn't stop Blake from ordering food from the nearest diner for her.

"I'm Enzo. I'm rarely proven wrong, but I'm happy to be proven wrong by…" I pause waiting for her to tell me her name.

Her eyes cut to me. "I don't give anything away for free."

ALSO BY ELLA MILES

LIES SERIES:

Lies We Share: A Prologue

Vicious Lies

Desperate Lies

Fated Lies

Cruel Lies

Dangerous Lies

Endless Lies

SINFUL TRUTHS:

Sinful Truth #1

Twisted Vow #2

Reckless Fall #3

Tangled Promise #4

Fallen Love #5

Broken Anchor #6

TRUTH OR LIES:

Taken by Lies #1

Betrayed by Truths #2

Trapped by Lies #3

Stolen by Truths #4

Possessed by Lies #5

Consumed by Truths #6

DIRTY SERIES:

Dirty Obsession

Dirty Addiction

Dirty Revenge

Dirty: The Complete Series

ALIGNED SERIES:

Aligned: Volume 1

Aligned: Volume 2

Aligned: Volume 3

Aligned: Volume 4

Aligned: The Complete Series Boxset

UNFORGIVABLE SERIES:

Heart of a Thief

Heart of a Liar

Heart of a Prick

Unforgivable: The Complete Series Boxset

ABOUT THE AUTHOR

Ella Miles writes steamy romance, including everything from dark suspense romance that will leave you on the edge of your seat to contemporary romance that will leave you laughing out loud or crying. Most importantly, she wants you to feel everything her characters feel as you read.

Ella is currently living her own happily ever after near the Rocky Mountains with her high school sweetheart husband. Her heart is also taken by her goofy five year old black lab who is scared of everything, including her own shadow.

Ella is a USA Today Bestselling Author & Top 50 Best-selling Author.

Stalk Ella at:
www.ellamiles.com
ella@ellamiles.com

Made in the USA
Coppell, TX
31 January 2021

49250826R00127